Praise for NOTHING TO FEAR...

"A positive and powerful view of Y2K that even 'computer disadvantaged' people like myself can easily understand. The fact that it is embedded in an entertaining, fast-paced story makes it all the more enjoyable. *Nothing to Fear* makes it abundantly clear that Y2K is not about what computers will do; it's about what we will do."

John Barletta
United States Secret Service (Ret.)

"I thoroughly enjoyed *Nothing to Fear*. More than entertaining and informative, it also is loaded with suspense, humor, and a sense of spirituality—a combination readers don't often find. I learned a great deal from reading *Nothing to Fear*."

Kate Schwab
General Manager, Borders Books & Music
Santa Barbara, CA

"Jefferey Modic and Bayard Stockton have tackled a complicated issue with guts and humor. This is a clever, entertaining approach to Y2K, with a message that is right on target—common sense is always the best defense."

John L. Petersen
President, The Arlington Institute
Author of *Out of the Blue:
How to Anticipate Wild Cards and Big Future Surprises*

"In *Nothing to Fear* Jefferey Modic, a twenty-five-year veteran of Y2K, has given us an exciting account of what Y2K could eventually bring if the administration remains silent on the risks of Y2K and the need to prepare. *Nothing to Fear* is a wonderful and compelling medley of truth and fiction. A good read."

Steven C. Davis
President, DavisLogic, LLC
and coauthor of *Y2K Risk Management*

"Of all the leading experts I have interviewed about Y2K, I find Jefferey Modic has some of the best insights about how the American people perceive it. From the White House and Senate chambers in Washington to the town halls and main streets of Anytown, USA, *Nothing to Fear* weaves current events and fiction together into a compelling and provocative story of the Millennium Bug. Along the way, it raises powerful questions about government, the media, and corporate America that we will all be discussing long after Y2K is behind us."

Patrick D'Acre
Publisher of *Y2K Update Report*
"Sensible Insights from Responsible Experts"
http://www.y2kupdatereport.com

"For decades Jefferey Modic, as a respected authority on information management, has lived with the sound of that ticking clock moving us all toward the millennium and the challenge of Y2K. In *Nothing to Fear* he has combined high technology with politics and current events to give us an unsettling fictional account of the world he believes we may soon be facing. A timely reminder that January 1, 2000, may be only the beginning of a continuing challenge for us all."

Ed Joyce
Former president, CBS News

Because of a design feature in many electronic systems, a large number of activities in the public and private sectors could be at risk beginning in the year 2000.

President William J. Clinton
February 4, 1998
Executive Order 13073

The only thing we have to fear is fear itself.

President Franklin D. Roosevelt
March 4, 1933
First Inaugural Address

Nothing *to* Fear

Jefferey Modic
with
Bayard Stockton

Tom,
Thanks for all the great work and for your guidance for the folks on the front line.

JM

Tres Pinos Press
Tres Pinos, California

Published by: **Tres Pinos Press**
PO Box 1174
Tres Pinos, CA 95075

Editor: Ellen Kleiner
Book design and production: Richard Harris
Cover design and production: Richard Harris
Front cover photograph: Santa Ynez Valley by William Etling
Back cover photograph: Anne Heck

Copyright © 2000 by Jefferey Modic

All rights reserved. No part of this book may be reproduced in any form whatsoever without written permission from the publisher, except for brief quotations embodied in literary articles or reviews.

Nothing to Fear is a work of fiction. Any resemblance to persons living or dead is purely coincidental.

Printed in the United States of America on acid-free recycled paper

Publisher's Cataloging-in-Publication Data

Modic, Jefferey.
   Nothing to fear / Jefferey Modic ;
with Bayard Stockton. — 1st ed.
   p. cm.
   LCCN: 99-91015
   ISBN: 0-9672508-0-3

   1. Year 2000 date conversion (Computer systems)
—Fiction. 2. Computers and civilization—
Fiction. I. Stockton, Bayard. II. Title.

PS3563.O267N68 1999   813'.54
                         QB199-1400

10 9 8 7 6 5 4 3 2 1

This book is dedicated to:

Susan, Kate, and Daniel

Bettina, Jonah, Tam Austen, and their cousins yet to come

ACKNOWLEDGMENTS

Many people generously contributed their time and expertise so that this book could be written. I would like to acknowledge each and every one by name, but for lack of space I must thank all of you collectively. Whatever good comes from this book is largely due to you.

Formally, I wish to thank the following people for their insights and contributions:

US Senators Robert Bennett and Christopher Dodd, and the staff of the Senate Special Committee on the Year 2000 Technology Problem, for their magnificent job in providing detailed information on the impact of the year 2000 technology problem in the United States and abroad. US Congressman Steven Horn and the House Subcommittee on Government, Management, Information, and Technology for their report cards on the federal government's progress in repairing the year 2000 computer problem. US Congressman John Doolittle for giving me the opportunity to contribute to the war on the Millennium Bug at the federal level, and California State Senator Tim Leslie for providing that same opportunity at the state level. Mr. John Koskinen and the staff of the President's Council on the Year 2000 Conversion for candidly sharing, "what they knew, as they knew it."

Dr. Ed Yardeni for providing some of the boldest economic insights of his career, when he could have played it safe. Dr. Forest "Woody" Horton Jr., for his sage counsel and Washington insight. And H. Ross Perot for showing me how God, duty, honor, family, and country can and should exist in the boardroom.

Peggy Keller for always being there to lend steadfast support and to offer her expert advice. I am lucky to be associated with her. Ellen Kleiner and Richard Harris for their unfailing assistance, editorial guidance, artistic talents, and doses of literary reality. Barbara DeSantis for her excellent media guidance, excitement, and enthusiasm. Patrick D'Acre for his creative insights and for decoding the spin. Duane Unkefer and Georgia Bertin for their heroic efforts in the final days. Kate Schwab for her advice and support. Patricia Murphy, Diane de Avalle-Arce, Maggie Hartley, Pat Mitchell, and Academic Ann for reading and commenting on the manuscript in its early stages. Robert Wilmott for working on early cover designs. Bayard's adult education writing class for their support during the many preliminary read-throughs. And especially Bayard Stockton, without whom this novel would not have been written.

In keeping with saving the best for last, I thank my wife Susan and our children, Kate and Daniel—my true sources of inspiration for this book.

CHAPTER ONE

Santa Ynez Mountains, California
June 1999
Fumes from the fifty-five-gallon fuel drums nearly overpowered Mark Steinhart. Sweat stung his eyes. He went outside for a deep breath of cleansing pine from the surrounding forest. A broiling summer day down on the rolling floor of the Santa Ynez Valley. Even up here, well over 3,000 feet, only a listless breeze fanned the shimmering waves of heat.

The Steinharts had invested everything in surviving the coming chaos of Y2K, and Mark's inner clock kept track, almost down to the hour and minute. Now, just 225 days before Armageddon, the moments were ticking by far faster than he had anticipated. He was behind, according to his master schedule, but deliveries of the stuff they had to buy were often spotty and the drums had been cursedly hard to find. Mark winced and went back into the utility building to resume pumping. Just then, Ellen banged the old triangle on the tree near the cabin, signaling fifteen minutes to wash up before supper. They liked to eat early, to savor the sunset hours and enjoy a pleasant break in the punishing routine they had set for themselves and the kids.

Inside, the ranch house was an apple-pie scene. All the Steinharts, polished clean after the energetic day, were sitting around the California oak table Mark had crafted back at the old house in Menlo Park.

Mark glanced around at the three kids. He reached out his hands, waiting until the circle was complete at Ellen's end. Mark bowed his head, and let Spirit dictate his words of thanks. It was a Thursday, which meant silent meditation until after the salad. Mark reflected on the gratitude he had just expressed. Life here was so different from the world they had left, with its deceitful academic politics and shameful, ego-driven scrambling for recognition. Sharing his gloom, Ellen had founded the Pentecostal Redemption Church, and Armageddon had become a certainty in their lives. Mark had gone to some Promise Keepers meetings until the organization began to lose momentum. Then in 1996, both Mark and Ellen had taken early retirement bonuses and headed for blessed simplicity.

The Steinharts didn't break from the cyberworld all at once. First they had to find land that met their conditions for safety: limited access, protectability, water supply, gardening and grazing acreage—a place where they could build a defensive compound without drawing too much negative attention to themselves. And where they would be safe and secure on January 1, 2000.

They decided on the coastal range, where the climate wouldn't be too extreme. But not near Silicon Valley, which they thought might suffer the most wrathful revenge come The Millennium.

The Steinharts had enough money to buy their chosen land from Jim Martin, a reputable real estate agent down in Solvang. And now up here, they were on their own. No more fiddle-faddle, none of the time-wasting social and financial demands of Silicon Valley life.

Mark meditated again on the fruits of his labors. They had built the cozy ranch house almost entirely by themselves, with a few assists from local craftsmen they had met while still attending church or as a result of Jim Martin's recommendations. Now they were ready to withstand the onslaught of any season—from an El Niño rain, even snow, to the blistering heat that global warming brought these days.

They had all the basics, plus a bit of comfort. No air conditioning, of course, but swamp coolers and a gas-driven fridge, even a satellite dish and big-screen TV to watch football, basketball, and the Trinity network—at least until the national power grid gave out.

Ellen had taken the lead in placing their fate in the hands of God. She worked side by side with Mark, tilling the land to make productive gardens. Then she went further than they had planned: she bought bales of cotton and learned how to gin it, after which she found a hand-operated loom and taught herself to weave. When she'd made her first homespun cloth, the family laughed at her vegetable dyes. Now she was learning, from one of the many helpful sites on the Internet, how to fill tooth cavities. She had even volunteered to be the compound plumber.

They had long ago laid in plentiful stores of freeze-dried foods and fitted their well with an old-fashioned hand-pump. The chain-link fence that circled the property, right up to the National Forest line, had been a bear to put up, but it gave much-needed protection to the gardens, the growing fruit trees, the compost heap, chicken run, and the sheep and cattle. And of course the dynamite and weapons they'd need for the bad times ahead when acquaintances, Valley folk, or even people from the cities might come marauding in search of food and shelter. The only fear they recognized was fear of God and his wrath.

Out in the utility shed, the generator hummed. Thursday was the day all standby systems were programmed to run checks on themselves until they clicked off at 7:00 P.M. Thursday was also twelve-year-old Luke's day for kitchen duty. When he'd finished his salad, he clattered the plates in noisy protest until Ellen shushed him with a glance.

The brief glow of satisfaction Mark had allowed himself was dimmed by teenage Ruth, who still had an unfortunate tendency to whine despite talking-tos, even additional Scripture readings. "But

Dad, why can't I have any friends, like kids I could invite up here to sleep over? Not even Sunday School."

Mark and Ellen looked at each other, partly amused, partly in despair. They had been sure the kids would love the natural life as much as they did, but it hadn't worked out that way. At least not yet.

"The people down in town really think we're weird," Ruth went on. "I mean, the way you make me dress! Not even a tank top, like all the girls. It sucks! We're sort of like celebrities, y'know? I mean, who else down there has been on a program like *Nightscape?* That's almost like being on *60 Minutes!*"

Luke was feeling a bit squirrelly, too. "Yeah," he added, "what a rat's life!"

Ruth sensed it was time for a tactical retreat. "Could we see the tape again later on? You guys looked so *cool*. Real God-fearing."

Luke trampled roughshod over his sister's peace offering. "Yeah, right. And maybe I'd like to play ball with the guys down there."

Ellen admonished Luke with a glance that made him stiffen. "We'll see. After chores. You know we have to stick to the schedule." Then she said, as she had so many times before, "No more discussion! Just do as your father says and everything will be all right. We put our faith in the Lord, and he will provide."

Mark offered compromise. "How's about we have a bit of batting practice after table, son? You're rusty. Maybe we ought to work off some of those hormones rattling your cage, huh? Or if you're too tired to play with the old man, maybe a few chapters of Old Testament?"

Luke bowed his head over the sink, reprimand understood.

Then nine-year-old Lolly, who had been gauging the mood, chimed in. "My turn! You're going to check me out on the twenty-two, remember?" Lolly had quickly become a crack shot with the light rifle in only a few lessons. Her napkin slid to the floor. She picked it up, folded it on the table, then climbed onto Mark's lap to practice the wiles every daughter innately knows.

Ellen shot a look of admonition down the table. Time was being wasted.

* * *

Out in the storage wing, something else was happening . . .

When he'd heard the dinner triangle, Mark welcomed the break from his efforts to solve his ongoing fuel access problems, especially securing the manual pumps to get gasoline from the drums to his three vehicles. There were several near-empty drums; he'd lost track and neglected to replace the stoppers.

Earlier, he had noticed the strong gasoline smell, but wrote it off to minor fuel leaks in one of the vehicles or the gasoline-powered chain saw or riding tractor. When the garage doors were open, you could barely notice it. The doors were not open now; they had been closed all day . . . and the fumes had been collecting under the slant-roof, designed to direct heat to the vent fans he had planned to install the next week.

Further, the propane system, composed of pipes that delivered gas from the outside storage tanks to the various connections that provided hot water and heat to the house, had developed two leaks. Mark had installed the pipes himself, stood by as they passed official inspection, and then gone back and done more work on them. For ten days the propane had been seeping out. Odorless and heavier than air, the gas had saturated the loose earth beneath the raised foundation, filled the crawl space, and then, following gravity, flowed along the floor in an ankle-high, invisible tide into the storage area—where one case of TNT and the ammunition stores were locked away—and into the garage.

Further yet, Mark had neglected to cap one nearly empty—thus highly volatile—fifty-five-gallon drum of varnish, used to weatherproof the compound's many raw wood surfaces. While the Steinharts dined, these lighter-than-air fumes, heated by the soaring temperatures, had drifted upward and mixed with the gasoline fumes against the sloped ceiling, then crept over an unfinished partition that separated the storage area from the garage.

The main furnace was in the corner formed by this partition and the back wall. When the Steinharts began dessert, the furnace burner flared to life, as programmed, to test the system.

The first explosion in a series that would last six seconds blew out the back wall and the partition, igniting the second, which lifted the house off its foundation. Almost simultaneously, the fumes that had collected under the slant ceilings of the storage wing and garage exploded in a fireball of such violent force that both buildings and most of the house were consumed. Massive sections of flaming roof structure sailed in all directions.

The last one-two detonation—from the dynamite and the vehicles—leveled what was left, launching a second shower of flaming debris some 200 feet into the surrounding forest, paper-dry from a parched winter, setting it instantly aflame. Neither the Steinharts nor their animals drew a second breath.

It took a while for the Forest Service, sheriffs, and county fire department to maneuver their vehicles up to the Steinharts' secluded compound. As they did, they were closely pursued by the news truck from KSQK, the local network affiliate.

Novice reporter Gerri LaPorte—young, barely able to restrain her tears—almost whispered into her microphone. "The first victims of Y2K . . . months *before* the millennium! Remember when the Steinharts had the network cameras up here? And talked of their strategy for survival when Y2K . . ." Her cameraman had panned from a long shot of flames licking up the distant mountainside, back to the charred, still-smoking ruins where five bright blue plastic tarp-wrapped bundles were visible, two of them large and three small. Gerri let her microphone sag, as if it had become too heavy. "For survival . . . when . . . when . . ."

In the KSQK control room the news director spoke quietly into his anchor's ear. "Helen, Gerri's lost it. On my count . . ."

Helen Hope was calm, professional. "Back now in the studio . . . We'll return to Gerri as soon as she has more information for us on this terrible tragedy. Meanwhile, we want to remind you of how the Steinhart place looked when they opened their refuge to *Nightscape*'s cameras and spoke of their dreams."

The suave network interviewer and a confident, hospitable Mark and Ellen Steinhart chatted easily there just months ago—but they were suddenly preempted.

"This is Helen Hope again, at KSQK in Buellton, California. We have just learned this story is going out to the network, so let me recap: At five-forty-seven this evening, Pacific time, County nine one one received an emergency call from ranchers near Philip's Crest, in the Santa Ynez Range, saying they'd heard an explosion and could see a fire burning. Emergency Services responded and discovered the blaze had originated at the Steinhart compound, near the four-thousand-foot level, up at the head of the Valley, and from there it was spreading into Los Padres National Forest . . ." Helen clamped her earpiece tighter, and nodded.

"OK. Now we'll go back to our reporter, Gerri LaPorte, live at the scene. Stay tuned to 'The Eyes and Ears of the Santa Ynez Valley.'"

At network headquarters in New York, Herb Friedkin, a raspy old warrior, eyed a monitor and then hunt-and-pecked an e-mail to his subordinate editors: *California fire. high-profile community. first Y2K casualties angle. All progs—saturate—soft/hard! tx herb.*

Down in the Santa Ynez Valley, in the villages of Santa Ynez and Los Olivos, even on the outskirts of the tourist magnet, Danish-themed Solvang, many heard the rolling explosions, muffled by the miles of forests and field between the Steinhart compound and the towns, but resonating stronger again as they bounced off Lake Cachuma, the area's sprawling, multifingered reservoir.

Jim Martin and his teenage daughter, Kate, hastened out of their house and looked east toward the mountains. In the early twilight, they could make out nothing unusual. Then they heard the sirens as emergency vehicles roared along the highway toward the reservoir. Back inside, they watched KSQK as they continued to wash up after supper.

Jim quelled a sting of guilt over selling the property to the Steinharts a few years before, then wondered whether the fire might race out of control down into the Valley. The weather vane was listless. Jim figured the fire department would draw a containment line at the head of the Valley, above the reservoir.

Kate was anguished. "Oh, no! Ruth was my friend . . . at church day-camp last year. She didn't socialize much, till the end. But by then . . ." Her sentences came out in stutters. "I only saw her . . . a couple of times since . . . Once I saw them at 31 Flavors, like it was a really big deal."

KSQK had cut back to the *Nightscape* tape. The reporter's voice was rich. "The Steinharts built this compound over the last two years with their own sweat, and even some blood. It was the ultimate refuge for people who were convinced that December thirty-first, nineteen ninety-nine, will be the end of the world as we know it." Then he added dryly, "Most agree that this was an unusual reaction to the threat of Y2K . . ."

KSQK's livecam pictures of glowing embers and black-and-gray devastation again swept the screen. Gerri LaPorte came back on—soot-stained, obviously shaken—crouching behind the KSQK live truck. "Here's Howard Brown from the Forest Service to give us an update on the damage sustained . . ."

Kate turned to her father. "There's more to this Y2K thing than, like, what you've told me, isn't there? It's what you do—all the travel and the meetings! But you don't know how to fix it, do you?"

Jim shook his head, hurt by the anxiety in his daughter's voice. "It takes more than what any one guy can do. I can't fix it myself. No one can. We've done all we could possibly do, and we can't change the fact that too many people waited till the last minute because they didn't take it seriously, prepare for it. " He paused, distraught. "It's just too goddamn late." Knowing he shouldn't curse in front of his daughter, he added, "Sorry."

"I *know* all that, Daddy. Like you've told me a million times."

"Sweetheart, you shouldn't be worrying about this, not at your age. Everything will be fine."

Kate wiped her nose on her sweatshirt sleeve. "I'm not a little kid anymore, Daddy. I just don't understand how what happened to the Steinharts was caused by the Y2K thing."

"Well," Jim sighed, "in a way, Y2K did cause it to happen, indirectly, because the Steinharts were afraid of it . . . and they didn't need to be. They didn't get enough information. Because of fear, they stored up all kinds of dangerous things, like gasoline and dynamite and guns. Then something caused the explosion, an accident, and we don't know why yet . . ."

He reached out and cuddled his daughter, then went on. "But we're going to be OK, right? Trust me. Because we know what to do, and what not to do. It's just a matter of good old common sense. We haven't got gasoline and dynamite in our garage now, do we?"

The phone rang, and Kate leaped for it as usual. It was for her, as usual. She listened, covered the mouthpiece, looked over to him. "Daddy, it's Sandy. She was Ruthie's friend. Some other girls are over there and she wants me to come. Her mom will pick me up."

Saddened even more, her father nodded.

Jim leaned against the railing upright of his porch, queasy with horror. Although he hadn't known the Steinharts very well, they had made an impression on him: a straight-up American family, polite, smart, clean-cut. Sure, he'd been unable to buy into their apocalyptic vision of the new millennium, complete with marauding bands of hunger-crazed city people ravaging the countryside. Their religion wasn't his, either, but that made no nevermind. He couldn't keep their faces from crowding in on his thoughts. Had they tried to escape? Did they suffer terribly? What in God's name could have happened?

Along the mountains that chained the western horizon, he watched banks of brown-tinged haze float upward in the air currents, coloring the sunset a murky amber-orange. A great bank of purple and whitish-charcoal clouds stretched for miles to the east. One of the familiar red-and-white fire-bombers dived fearlessly into the stifling pall. Two helicopters, dangling 300-gallon buckets of water from Lake Cachuma, clattered overhead, making the ground tremble. It reminded him of war movies.

The light bar on the approaching Explorer told Jim it was Sheriff Mike Propoulos. A tunneling billow of grit followed, then overtook the vehicle, blew across the porch, and passed on. Mike pulled to an easy stop, and slumped behind the wheel as he talked into the car's hand mike. When he finished, he climbed out and stretched. Jim noticed his normally starched uniform was dusty and sweat-stained at the armpits.

"Evenin', Jim," Mike said.

"Sheriff. How's it going?"

"We've done about as much as we can for now. Got a minute?"

"Looks like you could use a cold one. Come on in."

"Yes to the beer, but I could also use a wash-up, and I'm not fit to come inside anywhere. Patty would kill me." Sheriff Mike's smudged hand brushed his thighs, raising wisps of ash that hung in the stillness of twilight. Grimy sweat-lines etched his thinly mustached face.

Jim slipped unconsciously into the easygoing conversational style he had absorbed since coming to the Valley years earlier. "Patty knows damn well you work harder than any other two guys on your force. Maybe this time she'll turn the hose on you before she lets you in the house. But here . . . You know where the bathroom is."

The sheriff moved stiff-legged into the house. When he came back out on the porch, Jim handed him a frosty-green bottle of Beck's and clutched his own favorite, an iced-tea-and-lemonade mix, biding his time. Propoulos—barrel-chested, one of the most powerful men in the county, and accustomed to going at his own pace—leaned against a pillar and pulled on the beer.

"Hell of a scene," Mike said finally. "Keep telling myself it's what I'm getting paid for." He stared off at the hazy sunset. Jim didn't want to imagine what he'd had to deal with up there.

"Never knew what hit 'em," Mike continued. "They were all pretty much in the same place . . . kitchen most likely, or dining room. Not a wall left standing. Arson investigators say it was probably fumes that sparked off. Gasoline drums, propane, maybe even dynamite. God-awful crater in the middle of it all . . ." The crusty sheriff's red-etched eyes roamed the surreal cloud banks.

The pause drew out, then Propoulos pulled himself back into his official role. "Reason I stopped by was, I gotta ask some questions. Not much left to go on up there. Figured you'd prefer me to one of the arson people."

"Whatever, Mike."

"There was enough wreckage up there for three houses. Looked like he'd built a goddamn fort." Propoulos rubbed the back of his neck while he talked. "How many times have you seen Steinhart since he moved up there?"

"Once in a while, in town, just passing. Kate knew his kids, but she never went up there. Never invited."

"Any ideas about what he was doing?"

"No more than any of us. He and that wife of his were scared witless by Y2K. Figured it was going to be doomsday. But you know that anyway." Jim scratched his chin. "They were reclusive, wanted everyone to respect their privacy. I always figured it was more him than her, but I butted out. Just 'Hello, how are you?' kind of stuff. Said they loved the place. That's all . . . Mike, you angling for something? If so, spit it out."

Sheriff Mike took another draft from the bottle, rocked a little on his boot heels, and looked keenly at Jim. "Well, yeah. You get an explosion like that these days, the first thing comes to mind is a meth lab. People blowing themselves up all over the place, making crack and those other drugs."

Jim rattled the ice cubes in his glass, realizing he now knew why Mike was so wrung out by the fire. The guy had spent several years working with Patty Propoulos's orphaned nephew, almost like a father, trying to heal the boy's anger over the loss of his parents to a doped and drunken driver. Mike had taught him to ride and taken him fishing in the mountains, but the boy had given in to a darker calling and slipped into the drug underworld. Then one day, Patty

Propoulos's nephew had blown himself and his girlfriend up in a meth lab explosion.

"Reason tells me," Mike continued, "people like the Steinharts wouldn't be into something like that. Just checking."

"Honestly, Mike. You think I wouldn't have told you if I'd known? I hate the thought, just like you do." For one of the few times in his life, Jim was testy. "OK, sorry. I know, you gotta do your job. But no, I for sure don't think the Steinharts would've been into that stuff. Period!"

Mike nodded again. "I read you. Nowadays, we got guys like him popping up all over. Hauling their wife and kids off to the boonies. Second Coming. But some of them . . . Well, you just never know. We're calling it an accident. Still, it's real hard to figure out how it happened. Goddamn flash-fried chicken all over the place . . . Funny part is, it smelled good." The sheriff shook his head. "But nothing else did . . ."

"I'll call you if I think of anything, Mike. And I'll check with Kate."

When Sheriff Propoulos got to his vehicle, he turned around. "Remember that chat we had last summer about this Y2K business? I found out Steinhart paid Patty's cousin over in Buellton real well to teach them how to handle a bunch of weapons. Had himself a small arsenal . . . Think we're going to see more Steinharts?"

"Hope not, Mike."

"I hope not, too. But do you think we will?"

"Yessir, Mike," Jim came back, straight as always, "I do. And I think there may be more than we reckon up there in the Los Padres."

Mike nodded agreement. "That's what I hear."

"The feds are saying everything's under control, when they should have been telling everyone to get prepared. They've created a complacency, which could boomerang. People know they're being lied to, but they're concentrating on other things right now—which means too many of 'em will get panicky at the last minute, just before New Year's."

The sheriff climbed into the Explorer. "That's what I figured. Anything you and your Y2K bunch can do about it?" Mike Propoulos left the question hanging as he wheeled away from Manzanita Ranch.

Jim held on to the railing, watching Mike's dust recede. Then he made a fist and began to pound the rail. *Beth . . . Oh, Beth,* he thought. *I did all I could . . . and I'll keep on doing it, just like I promised. But I'm afraid we've waited too long. There may not be enough time, dammit!*

CHAPTER TWO

San Francisco Bay
February 1976
The aircraft carrier sliced out into the Pacific. Thousands upon thousands of tons of steel gliding elegantly under the Golden Gate Bridge—a picture of peaceful might as the waves curled past her bow and rippled along her flanks, melding into a wake of farewell as she headed off to join the Seventh Fleet on a tour of sentry duty around Japan, Korea, Taiwan. Hot spots, where war could break out at almost any instant and radically change the lives of those here at home. Jim Martin could discern the tiny figures of crewmen scurrying on the flight deck, making final preparations for the open sea. His military service hadn't looked even faintly that romantic.

He grew up in South Pasadena. His father retired as an LAPD lieutenant in Los Angeles's notorious 77th Division. His mother had come, as she often remarked, "from the hills of Kentucky." From the age of fourteen, Jim had worked in the sturdy, old-fashioned American way. And he'd never stopped. He did all the usual jobs—from newspaper routes to hamburger joints, and on up the scale to supermarket bag boy. Yet somewhere down deep, he'd always wanted to be a cowboy, be away from cities, riding the open range, free, and able to see the horizon. It would take a while yet, he now realized.

As the Vietnam War peaked, Jim, at seventeen, was already into computer programming at Pasadena's community college. Then he made his first well-timed move, signing on for four years in the Air Force, with plenty of high-tech training stipulated. With his hefty background in computers, he was assigned to Vandenberg Air Force Base on California's Central Coast, working with the computers that launched the awesome might of the Titan missile.

He logged his time as a five-stripe sergeant, often hunkered in subterranean control centers, training and preparing to carry out launch commands, hoping they wouldn't come yet psyched for war at a moment's notice. When he took his discharge in the spring of 1974 despite intense pressure to re-up, he had a nice, clean, promising, totally left-brained record.

Hodge Renk's Integrated Electronic Management Systems (IEMS) was new to the Fortune 1000, and it was strictly controlled out of Phoenix, Arizona. The company made a habit of combing the military for men who had thousands of dollars' worth of government-paid computer training, years of hands-on experience, and a take-no-prisoners attitude. Martin sailed through IEMS's three rounds of intensive interviews, the last with the lanky Arizonan himself. ("Pride myself I'm a good judge of character, boy. You got promise. Now, don't you go and let me down, hear?" Only Renk, whose profanity was legendary, didn't say it quite that way, Jim recalled.) Wearing Renk's stamp of approval, Jim was dispatched to San Francisco, surprised he hadn't had to swear another oath of allegiance.

The new systems engineer busted his butt on Advanced Medicare Information Systems, IEMS's revolutionary Medicare claims processing system developed for the Blue Diamond Insurance Company. This new program spat out Medicare reimbursement checks within a startling seven days—compared with the old system's thirty or forty days. By age twenty-six, Jim was project manager on the showcase system, and with a night school BS on his résumé, he had the makings of a model corporate man.

The carrier was barely a thumbnail on the horizon when Jim fielded a call from the Blue Diamond Medicare claims processing manager, Tom Cathcart. Social Security Agency (SSA) headquarters in Baltimore, the claims manager ranted, "has rejected another handful of critical and terminal claims. The folks in Baltimore refused to pay because their records show the beneficiaries are dead. And right now I got one of those mad-as-hell dead beneficiaries on hold!

"This guy's pissed! Not dead—*pissed!* Customer service bucked him to me. Says he has his twelve-gauge primed, locked, and loaded, threatening to come here and ventilate someone unless he's paid, like now. Says he has nothing to lose!"

Jim snapped to full attention. "Slow down, Tom!"

The manager's fear was palpable. "The medical providers have cut the poor bastard off because SSA refuses to pay. And he doesn't have the bucks. We keep telling Baltimore we know he's alive, and they keep telling us he's roadkill!"

"Alert security, just in case," Jim said, "and stall him." He worked his keyboard furiously. "Our guy's eligibility goes through year two thousand three, check? And we send them only 'oh-three' on the eligibility interface tape, right?"

"Not just him," Tom moaned. "I'm sitting on sixteen other unresolveds right now. I don't know what's going on here, but if we don't resolve it ASAP we could have a US senator breathing down our necks."

Jim's thoughts crystallized. "Gotcha! Baltimore's mainframe must think it's nineteen oh-three, not two thousand three. That's why it automatically rejected him." He felt a surge of triumph at his discovery. Let me talk to your guy. He's flipped you off already. He needs to know we're onto what's happening and we're going to bat for him. Topside."

Jim felt skittish, but eased the customer's frayed temper with the promise of an interim check right away. He crashed through the secretarial perimeter and into the office of the regional vice president of IEMS's West Coast operations, where he quickly sketched how he thought the century dates were being misinterpreted by Social Security's big IBM mainframe.

Bill Garofala grasped the baton quickly. The two conference-called Renk in Phoenix. He authorized them to fly to Baltimore to lay the problem out for Social Security headquarters and report back to him personally, ASAP.

That night they caught the red-eye from San Francisco to Baltimore. After an airport coffee-and-doughnut breakfast, they trotted through a labyrinth of halls to the office of Janet Montori, assistant director of Medicare Beneficiary Eligibility. Janet called in SSA's head of data processing. Then Jim and Bill walked the officials through their growing concerns.

Janet easily grasped the situation and turned to her computer expert, asking, "If we were to use all four digits of the year, could we eliminate the glitch?"

To her astonishment, her techie explained that the SSA mainframe was programmed to store only the last two digits of the year.

"Why?" Janet demanded.

"Back when the system was first designed, we thought we'd need seven percent more disk space to store the four-digit date. The cost-benefit people estimated it would take an additional hundred and twenty-five thousand dollars per year to buy the disk drives. And besides, in nineteen seventy the Bureau of Standards said two digits was official government policy. Word was, the Pentagon had some influence in the decision."

"You mean we created this mess just to save some pennies a few years ago?" Janet was aghast. "I spend ten *million* a *year* on computers!"

The techie grimaced. "Your predecessor had to choose between raises for his staff and additional disk drives for the computer. He figured two digits or four digits was no big deal. And the Bureau of Standards had set policy. Besides, he felt this system wouldn't be around by the year two thousand."

Janet breathed out hard, then calmed down. SSA simply didn't have the money it would need to fix the current systems. She was stunned at the irony, that lack of foresight prevalent in every department she tried so hard to prevent in her own. She didn't even dare to guess how many millions could have been saved if only . . .

Thinking of the angry client with the shotgun and the others, Garafola suggested, "Could you authorize interim payments? It may be literally life or death."

Janet's outer bureaucrat struggled with her inner human being. She nodded. "OK. I'll take the responsibility. It may blow my job evaluation, but let's hand-process the claims to pay those people soonest, like now!" She stood up. "If you guys will excuse me . . ."

Jim was gloomy on the afternoon flight back to the Pacific Coast. "If they keep those programs around another twenty-plus years, they'll have a real monster on their hands. Us, too."

"But that's how government works," Garafola replied. "There's no career upgrades in future-think. They bury the problem till the last minute. If reporters happen to get onto the story, they pass the buck to some other department or deny everything. There's no problem, never was, never will be. Or they spin it—like maybe it's terrorist fanatics. People buy anything."

When they reported back to Phoenix, Hodge Renk sniffed profit. He launched a hush-hush in-house research project, called it Operation Year 2000, and gave it the secret code designator Y2K—Y for year and 2K for two thousand—assuming nobody would ever figure it out. He then appointed Jim Y2K's project manager. Jim shut his office door in San Francisco and began to evaluate the paralyzing potential of the double-zero problem. If what he suspected was actually fact, this Y2K baby could have terrifying consequences. Once he got into the real code-unscrambling, the number-crunching work, he was truly scared by the consequences he could envision as the dating snafu wormed its way through the ever-growing number of computers. The consequences were indeed so complex as to be unimaginable.

Simultaneously, Jim got Renk's clearance to attend day classes at Berkeley so that he could keep up to speed with the latest technology—and earn a master's degree in systems management as well.

Berkeley, California
Spring 1976

Jim always tried to look spit-and-polished and neatly creased, the way Mr. Renk liked his associates to be. White or light-striped oxford shirt, regimental striped tie, and a dark suit. But somehow the crease in Jim's pants never lasted—he often came across as though he'd slept at the office. At twenty-six, he knew he sometimes looked more like the ruin of a man of thirty going on forty. In spite of his schedule, he made time to keep in shape, often jogging early in the morning or late in the evening. Occasionally working out at a nearby gym.

Sometimes, not often, he thought of his personal life. He had a great apartment in the lower Berkeley foothills, which he all too seldom enjoyed. No time for girls. What woman wanted a guy who spent his time romancing computers? He appraised his looks. Handsome? Not really. Average. Well, maybe a tad better than average. Six-four wasn't too tall—same as Mr. Renk. Good pecs. Abs not bad. Didn't smoke. Didn't care much for booze. Just like Hodge. Jim checked for wrinkles.

Then sure enough, there was a little clump of wet hair in the teeth of his comb. "So, where does all the clean living get me? Life's out of balance," he said to himself. The face in the mirror looked back. "You gotta get out there, live normally. And you gotta start making some real money. Then you can run your own life. And stay in shape."

Next time he was at the gym, Jim surveyed it with the cunning of an experienced beach bum. Among the ranks of attractive women, his attention was drawn several times to a tall, not-too-stringy brunette. He could have sworn she'd looked in his direction, maybe even twice. Yes, she was aware of him, for sure. Maybe she was just shy, old-fashioned, not forward. In this day and age? He liked that!

No one had ever taught Jim how to hit on a girl with finesse. *How the hell do I make an approach without looking like I want to get in her pants right this minute?* She looked so together. *Damn! Can't look dumb.*

He asked a trainer for her name.

"Beth Oldfield," the trainer replied. "But hey, man, take it easy. It could cost me my job to give out personal information."

"Know anything about her? Off the record."

The trainer looked around, then muttered, "Not much. Grad student. Biology, maybe botany. Too bad. She's too good-looking to be an academic, that's for sure."

Just then, Beth Oldfield glanced over at the two men and quickly looked away with the hint of a smile. The men turned their backs, trying not to appear furtive.

"Oh damn!" Jim mumbled.

"So what?" The trainer shrugged. "Just go for it! Ask if she's attached. And maybe she'd like to go for a coffee? Show you got the old *cojones*, man!" He strolled away, grinning at Jim's inhibitions.

Jim let the concept bubble for a week, then late one afternoon he figured he was as psyched as he'd ever be. He didn't get on a machine, but went right over to Beth, feeling as graceful as an elephant. He was instantly dissolved by the warmest smile he could have imagined. "Hi. I've been watching you. I mean . . ."

"Hi, I know. Don't worry . . ." She stumbled too, in sync with his shyness. "I heard . . . you're Jim. I asked." Her words bounced like Ping-Pong balls from a lottery basket.

"You did? So did I . . ." *Oh man, what now?* Long, toe-curling pause. "Well, how's about a cup of tea? Figure you're not a coffee person." If Jim could have scuffed his toes, he would have.

Beth helped. Was she as eager as he was? She seemed so cool. "Do we have to play hopscotch? I mean, we could really go now. I'm nearly done. Oh, but you haven't . . ." Beth backed-and-filled neatly. "Half an hour?"

They went for decaf and herbal tea, and exchanged backgrounds, at which point Jim figured he just might have found that special girl. There was so much to her . . . so much to discover. He walked her home, then barely touched ground as he made his way back to his apartment. He had her phone number. And she'd said it was OK to call.

There were very long phone calls over the next few days, so many that Beth finally said, "Enough! You don't leave me time to hit the books!" But she offered compensation, in the form of a bold hint. She mentioned that a movie she wanted to see was playing in San Francisco. Jim quickly issued the invitation.

They caught the subway, saw the film, strolled into Chinatown. Her hand brushed his. He seized the chance.

They ambled on, gawking at dried fish and the weird vegetables; grinning over feathery noodles and yukky-looking mushrooms in the dry goods stores. They ogled the knock-off copies of Western products; did their own takeoffs on the tourists slinging and unslinging their cameras, constantly checking to make sure their wallets were still in hip pockets, their purses still at the ends of their straps.

The two turned into a small restaurant away from the glitzy lights, fumbled with chopsticks, and snuggled shoulder to shoulder on the BART back to Berkeley. Jim walked Beth to her house.

There came the moment of high schoolish embarrassment. Beth one step above, now equal in height to Jim. Very close. Jim working hard to stifle his breathing. A two-second megapause.

Finally, "Well, good night, Jim. I really enjoyed the evening with you, and thank you."

"You're welcome. Me too."

"I'd like to invite you in . . ."

He shrugged mutely, waited, tense. She was letting him sweat up a storm.

Beth continued, calm, "I'm very attracted to you. But I think we ought not to rush things."

"Absolutely. No. Me too. Sure. OK."

"But I do want to see you again." Beth leaned into him. Their lips brushed, then locked. Jim's arms went around her of their own accord, squeezing hard, as if operating on remote.

She pulled away, a bit breathless but smiling. "My mom always said, 'Don't kiss on the first date,' and look at me now."

Jim, puffing, crashed through her verbal obstacles. "Gym next week? And I'll call . . . tomorrow OK? I don't want to push you too hard."

"Sure. I don't think Mom would mind. Just leave me time to study, is all."

Mostly they went to movies, sometimes a play at Berkeley Rep. Grateful Dead concerts at the Oakland Coliseum turned Beth on, although she always refused the pot that circulated there so freely. Jim remained a somewhat starchy observer of The Dead's revels, unable to unbend as much as the people all around them.

At home, one cooked dinner for the other, although except for his specialty of jalapeño spaghetti sauce, it was mostly lopsided: Beth cooked and Jim watched. Gradually, tentatively, they progressed to petting, no more. Whenever it got too hot and heavy, edging right up to the brink, Jim felt he had to back off. He wanted to save lovemaking for when they were more committed to each other, perhaps getting ready to live together. Beth seemed to feel the same way, only she was bolder. Also, he reminded himself, she really got hot pretty easy.

Trouble was, they were so deeply hooked into their career goals they could hardly begin to think of a future together. The more Jim compared his work on Operation Y2K with his romance with Beth, the more he realized he'd basically been leading a hermit's life. Was he repressing his normal feelings? Was he hiding in armor too rigid to bend? Too protective of his carefully circumscribed world to allow a woman into his life? Beth was beginning to show him so many other aspects of things, of nature, of living. And there was promise of more revelations to come. Or, he wondered, were they just two career-track people destined to run along separate but parallel lines and never hit a junction?

What to do about this woman who had become so much a part of his routine? He had never opened up like this before. Neither in high school nor on his occasional brief flings in the Air Force. Not that he was a prude. Jim pretty much knew his way around with women. That's why he wondered why he was so nervous. If he went for her, would he be spending less time on Y2K? What about his career? And that money he wanted to make—stock options, retirement? Were they all compatible?

He couldn't help but recognize that with Beth he talked freely and honestly about everything—things he'd never before thought of mentioning. The stars. Jellyfish. Amoebas. Gerry Ford. The economy. Dreams. Careers. Frogs. And Y2K.

The phone rang. Hodge Renk's strangely squeaky voice oscillated down the line from Phoenix. "Pack your bags. You're coming down here."

"Say what . . . sir?"

"Two days oughta be enough to settle up. Be here, ready to work, Monday."

"Monday morning?" Jim fumbled, then said, "Yes, sir."

"Good promotion, you'll see. Deserve it, too. Daddy used to say, 'Allus reward loyalty.'"

"Promotion, sir?"

"Chief of Information Systems for IEMS. How's double your current salary, profit sharing, and stock options grab you?"

"Fine, sir. Fine. Thank you. I'll be there. Monday morning."

Overwhelmed that he had been recognized, Jim dropped the phone into its cradle. Then he quickly picked it up again, got Hodge's chief of staff, and negotiated a one-week delay before reporting in to head office. He cleared out his desk and ignored offers of a farewell drink.

On the way home, his mind reeled. Beth still had a year to go on her doctorate. And her dream was to teach at a top-drawer university like Berkeley. He dialed from his apartment. She answered in her I'm-studying-so-this-better-be-important mode.

"Gotta see you, honey."

"You sound upset."

"Half an hour?"

When he climbed the steps, the door was open. She came into his arms. A deep hug, lingering kiss. "OK," she said. "Good news, bad news?"

He smiled and said, "I could use a beer." Then he bounced from confusion to embarrassment. Beth hadn't had time to put on a bra under her T-shirt and her nipples were visible. She handed him a cold beer, eased down next to him, hipbone to hipbone, took his hand in hers, and held it in her lap. She lifted her bottle to clink against his.

"OK, fess-up time . . . Find another woman? You're sorry? Tell all!"

"No way. Being transferred to Phoenix. Immediately. Direct order from Hodge himself. Big promotion. Big money. But I got a week's delay."

Beth let out a breath. "Jim, that's what you've been working for! Only . . ."

"Yeah. Only . . ." He finished her thought with, "What about us?"

She took his Heineken from him. Then she put an arm around him, kissed him passionately, her mouth open, and guided his hand under her T-shirt. "Touch me, Jim," she whispered. "I want you. Now."

"But I thought we . . ." Jim felt the heat rising in his face.

"That was then; this is now. Things just changed. You'll be leaving. I'll be staying."

She led him into the bedroom. Beth proved surprisingly, enchantingly adept as a lover, demanding what she needed of Jim and giving herself totally to him.

Jim lay, still naked, cradling her in his arms. Replete. The lovemaking had been superb. He was surprised at the passion, even the ferocity Beth unleashed as she responded to him. And now, only moments later, the pragmatist was back in the saddle, his computer brain synchronizing in and out with her naturalist brain.

"Well, did that help anything?"

Beth recoiled. "*Help* anything? My God, no! It wasn't *supposed* to. Excuse me." She got up and pulled a wrap over her lithe torso, leaving the room.

Jim was mystified. What was this all about? "Beth," he called. "Hey! Don't go away like that." He started after her, then went back for his shorts and, hobbling, pulled them up as he followed her. "I don't want to go to Phoenix without you!" In the hallway he paused, still tugging at his boxers. What did he just say? "But I know you've got to stay here to finish your dissertation," he added, lamely.

Beth leaned against the kitchen doorjamb, flushed from passion, anger, even laughter at the sight of Jim with his shorts at half-mast. Composing herself, she began, "I never thought I'd hear myself saying what I'm going to say now, but . . . Let's just have this one week together. Then you go to Phoenix and I'll get back to work."

"One week? And that's it—good-bye?" He was stunned, but after a moment, it didn't seem such a radical idea. "OK. What'll we do?"

"Leave that to me."

And so it was. A week of bliss . . . which didn't fully work, because the tension grew worse as the deadline loomed closer. They acknowledged the strain was too much, separated briefly, and came together once more. Then Jim took the shuttle to the airport, not knowing if he would ever see her again. They were bitter-sad moments as the van hurtled toward South San Francisco. Yet also, moments of anticipated fulfillment of a different kind.

CHAPTER THREE

Phoenix, Arizona
June 1976

Phoenix's searing June weather wasn't auspicious for someone from the fog and breezes of the Bay Area, but Jim barely noticed it. He checked into the turquoise-tinted high-rise and was immediately taken to an airlock of a room to be briefed on IEMS security procedures. Then a polyester minion showed him to a corner office in the tower, and said if he wanted anything to "just press button A."

Jim scanned the vista of an air-conditioned city pushing fast out into the desert, adjusted the executive chair to his height, peered into drawers, and logged on to the computer. There he got another in-house welcome message, plus all the information he'd ever need about Phoenix: where IEMS thought you should live, the recommended golf and country clubs, where to buy American cars at a company discount, and where to rent horses.

In less than twenty minutes, a stern female voice summoned him up to the sanctum. Unaware that there were top-sergeantlike Arizonan women, he had to swallow his smile as he was trotted into Renk's suite.

The chief rose to his full six-foot-four-and-one-eighth inches, just a fraction above Jim's eye level. Height dominance established, Hodge pressed Jim's hand, folded back into his cowhide-covered chair, propped his iguana-skin boots on the highly polished manzanita wood desk, and smiled. Jim wondered if Hodge had a special low platform installed behind the desk to make him even taller.

Hodge Renk told inquirers, including those who didn't ask, that the heels on his handcrafted boots placed him even closer to the Guy Upstairs. "Sorta like having preferred customer access, y'know." The way he said it, it was not a spiritual assertion, but pecking-order, chain-of-command positioning.

Welcome-on-board formalities, forty seconds max. The nitty-gritty took a bit longer. The personal briefing was simple, and it became even clearer during the top-level department heads' meeting that immediately followed. Jim was now in charge of all IEMS information management systems. Under him was a platoon of hotshot computer troops. Above him, only one echelon of seniority. But, the Hodge said, his door was always open if a major question arose, especially on policy.

Renk told Jim and the CEO to stay on after the introductory meeting. "Don't want to get too many people involved," Renk explained. When the others had left, he went on. "Restructuring your job so you can spend as much time as you need chasing down this Y2K problem—gotta be our top priority. Work like you're always on red alert. Your deputy is gonna take most of the day-to-day load off you. He's cleared on a need-to-know basis only. Got that?"

"Yes, sir," Jim replied calmly.

"We play this one very, very close. Vest-pocket close . . . *Comprende, compañero?* You spot someone you like the looks of and you holler. To me only. You don't make a pitch to him—shucks, these days he could even be a her, I guess. You clear it through me. We keep this thing in-house tight." Hodge made it sound as if they were working inside a vault. "When we have enough stuff, we go to Washington, high-level. First class. Front door."

The chief paused, smiled thinly, then went on. "Meanwhile, don't talk to the Social Security people—or no one else—about it. No way. Not without Daddy present, understood?"

"Understood, sir."

"OK. Expect great things of you. Picked you myself, right outta the Air Force. Snapshit sergeant, and now you're making almost as much as the president, plus bennies. Not bad, huh? Knew you were a comer. Expect you to be a player. Got that? You're my tiger, remember that! Keep me posted, personally."

The bark of dismissal was abrupt: "Now, get outta here. Got work to do. Someone's gotta make some money around here!"

Only now, as Jim did a snappy about-face, did he realize that the entire time he had been standing at attention, thumbs at the seams of his new suit-pants.

Six months after Jimmy Carter was sworn in on the steps of the US Capitol, Jim Martin knew beyond a doubt that the nation, indeed the world, could face a crisis of unimaginable scale as it slid past January 1, 2000—unless hard decisions and major steps were taken well in advance. But could he persuade anyone other than the Hodge that he wasn't way off base? Renk was a moody, often taciturn mentor, always on the job. Yet, as he flayed Jim, he also taught him.

During the next year, Jim occasionally flew to Washington on the Renk family Gulfstream. Sometimes he traveled with others on a Learjet from the corporate pool; still pretty comfy. Other times he had to fly commercial. Once in the capital, he'd periodically recognize a fellow believer in Y2K and have a chance for a quiet, off-the-record chat. Jim began to pick up wispy trails of a growing Millennium Bug awareness in government—whispered hints that the guys he met knew something was wrong and nothing was going to correct the key flaw. When he asked why, he got only a blank stare.

All the while, he became familiar with congressional procedures, and acquainted with the halls and byways on the Hill. He absorbed lessons in how to get things done in the labyrinthine federal bureaucracy, which buttons to push in which agencies, and which senatorial or congressional offices needed occasional reminders of previous largesse so that Renk's people could gain access to key movers and shakers when needed.

Jim knew he was being brought along, like a minor league baseball player up for his first season in the smoke. Sometimes he even wondered if he had his name and a number stuck on his back. Relief pitcher? Shortstop? Where did he fit on Renk's all-star team? What was he being groomed for? It was an awkward and awesome thought.

Hodge had had a son, but the boy was killed learning to fly at age seventeen. It was a subject never mentioned at work. Renk's two daughters, who dropped by the office from time to time, were alert, sharp, even decorously flirtatious, but more interested in ranching or fashion retailing than in computers. Jim occasionally allowed himself to muse about whether Hodge might be looking for a husband for one or the other, then quickly dropped the idea. Managed marriage was not for him. Anyway, there was Beth—remote but still tantalizing, and very much on his mind. If only he could get over the awkwardness he felt when the urge hit him to call her again, to see if maybe they could get together, just one more time.

But here and now he was wired into his chilled office, a neat box in the table of organization. His world was name badge, rank, and perks. He knew the boss enough to call him Hodge, as did everyone else. And no one ever went by a nickname. Paranoia oozed downward in the IEMS tower.

Jim wished he could dress like he wanted to. But you never knew when the Man might call; it could even be at 2:00 A.M. So it was strictly by the book, every day—white shirt and dark conservative tie.

He had met a handful of people who, like himself, spent all their days and many nights at their screens, occasionally sleeping under their desks, existing on Cokes and coffee and Fritos from the machines down the hall, or maybe a medium-cold hot dog or a call-in pizza.

There was sometimes a beer with the guys at one of the bars in downtown Phoenix, or an occasional cookout in Scottsdale. Period.

Jim's world was mechanical, technological. Did he have real human contact? Even animal contact? He wanted a dog, but knew he wouldn't be home to feed the animal regularly. Nevertheless, Jim sensed instinctively the questions that haunted everyone at IEMS: How long before I'm of no more use to Hodge? When do I burn out and go into the discard? When is he going to find someone younger, quicker, brighter to replace me?

September 1977 rolled around. Sometimes Jim would catch a few minutes of a big football game. One weekend, Hodge declared a company holiday when the Arizona State Wildcats, the Arizona University Sundevils, and the fledgling Phoenix Cardinals all had make-or-break matchups. Big spread out at the family ranch. Mandatory show-face event. Casual dress, preferably from a local saddlery. Band and look-but-don't-touch cheerleaders brought in from the Flagstaff school one of the daughters went to. A whole steer, roasted on a spit by a passel of Mexican vaqueros.

Did Hodge try to push him and one of the daughters together? Was he fantasizing or nightmaring? Who knew what went through that contorted mind? Jim did chat with the more alert of the two Renkettes, but the old phrase "Don't dip your pen in the company inkwell" looped through his mind and he wandered away.

After three beers and a near lurch at one of the cheerleaders, Jim deemed he would be best advised to can it. Renk had provided chauffeured limos to pick up and return the hired help. Only later did it dawn on Jim that this was just another way the boss could keep tabs on his extended family. But it sure was a hell of a spread!

Berkeley
October 1977
It must have been the effect of the barbecue. Even though the entire affair had been meticulously staged, and everyone had played their part, Jim felt somewhat social for the first time in a long while.

Noticing his lonesomeness creeping up on him again brought his yearning to be with Beth back from the bleak abyss of denial to which he had consigned it.

Ever security-conscious, he loaded up with quarters, drove out to a pay phone, well away from anywhere a colleague might spot him, and dialed Berkeley. "I was thinking. Maybe we could see each other again, like over Thanksgiving?" He stumbled on. "I thought maybe up in the wine country. Or we could do Vail . . . if you want. Beth?"

"Hey, you caught me off balance. Can I call you back, maybe this evening? I don't feel too great taking personal calls at the office. And, well, we didn't do so good last time."

"Sure, but think about it, huh? And besides, I miss you." He smiled again, wondering if his words would surface on Renk's tape recorders.

She met him at the airport. Beth was in a hell of a hurry, so Jim co-piloted all the way over the Bay Bridge, hitting the brakes often. Once back at Beth's house, they made love, recklessly. Then they caught up.

Beth had become increasingly involved with environmental research and with the discovery of obscure plants that could help humankind. Her beat included the Upper Amazon, New Guinea, and Botswana. Collecting samples, she sweated in rain forests, got into mud up to her knees. She dealt with shamans and spirit speakers. She talked to biochemists in giant pharmaceutical houses; and she hung out with fringe people in the Bay Area who were sure herbs could cure all manner of illnesses. She started to appear at learned—and not so learned—conferences, discussing biodiversity, sustainability, even ethnobotany, subjects that left Jim challenged, and slightly uneasy.

But the weekend was just for them. Beth had laid in provisions: a duck instead of turkey, but all the trimmings; great Chardonnays and Cabernets from Napa and Santa Ynez; and pumpkin pie with her own hard sauce. It was a feast of provender—and of passion. Each consciously shut out the world they inhabited daily, to absorb each other. Gone were the hesitations, the fears of self-exposure and revelation. Beth made it so easy, so comfortable.

On Saturday they hiked up to Tilden Park, above Berkeley, and strolled around the wooded lake. Beth had brought a blanket; Jim's rucksack was full of choice tidbits. He held up a bottle. "A noble Loon Pond with some elegant pretensions?"

She laughed in throaty invitation. "The wine will keep. I have other needs. Come here."

And they rolled, wrestled, laughing until Beth pulled away and sat up. "My dear sir! Out here in the open air? Are your intentions honorable?"

"Uh-oh, I guess we ought to face it, huh?"

Beth smiled tentatively. "Was that a proposal?"

"Well, it's not like I haven't thought about it, but—"

"Hush! Don't sweat it. The way we're headed now, it just wouldn't work, and we both know it." Cooler yet, she added, "Maybe we can get together in the future . . . if we both feel the urge."

Jim was stunned by her sudden change from wanton lover to practical career woman. There was silence, a moment of adjustment. Then he found his voice. "Yeah, well . . . we've shared a great time together, and I've sure learned a lot from you." *Oh, damn! That was the wrong thing to say. Patronizing?* He'd felt so close to her—yet now, suddenly so distant.

"Can we leave it at that?" Her question was soft, but definitive. "The sweet memories. An affair to remember."

Jim paused, tears pushing behind his eyes. "I guess so. I guess you beat me to it. You make it sound so rational, so sensible. And I guess I wasn't sure I wanted to be sensible. Not yet."

"Jim, do you want to fly back tonight? I don't want you to, but it's an option. If you would feel more comfortable."

"Yeah . . . Maybe that would be better."

Jim collected his stuff at the apartment. Beth offered to drive, but he preferred to taxi. The parting was filled with controlled emotion. Then Jim was in the cab, swaying back across the Bay, thinking, doubting. Realigning.

Two young surgeons on the fast track. Each climbing a ladder, doing career, going where they had to go. Beth had her dream slot in Berkeley, poking around a planet he knew hardly at all. And him, tracking disaster-in-the-making, wondering how he could help all the people who might be hurt by Y2K.

Yes, damn right! It was time to separate. He stifled tears. He wondered if Beth was crying. Or if she had gone right back to her books.

Phoenix
January 1978
Jim had obviously been rising in Hodge Renk's esteem despite his unsuitability as designated son-in-law. Over Jim's objections that the assignment was impossible, Hodge had asked him to produce an overview of the Millennium Bug effect in three stages: US national economy, US international trade, and global economic repercussions.

"Chief of Information Systems" was still Jim's cover designation. In reality, however, he was now head of a task force dispersed all over Renkdom, and he reported only to the Man. Jim protested that the mission was damn near impossible, far beyond his capabilities as a backroom computer wonk.

This time Renk overrode him. "Whatever it takes. Get Human Resources to buy some economists. Clear your new hires through me. Tell me what you get so we'll have something to show the bozos up on Capitol Hill. I want it all yesterday, but I'll give you three months, and that's generous."

Jim buckled down. Even at this early stage, scenario-building the extent of damage Y2K could cause in the world was a daunting exercise. In fact, even with the mainframe computing capacity Renk had at his disposal, predicting the ramifications of what might happen was impossible.

Domestically, the complications were staggering enough. A system that was not "remediated"—a term coming into use for rewriting the billions of lines of Cobol, Fortran, and RPG computer codes that would have to be corrected—could infect other systems. Even if one computer system was clean, another might be "dirty," as might one of the subsidiary systems. And all these software-based computer fixes did not begin to address the hardware-based complications that needed correcting. Four hundred billion computer chips were embedded in electromechanical devices around the world, often in places no one was aware of. Like the computer chip that controlled the output of petrochemical fertilizer plants. Or the microdevices that operated wastewater treatment plants. They would all need to be located, tested, and if necessary, repaired.

As for the global economy, it had not yet become inextricably interwoven, but indications were that it was heading that way. If one country that supplied the US was not in good shape, it could affect the American economy. Look at oil, for instance, Jim thought, and shuddered.

There was just too much information to input and absorb, too many permutations and imponderables, even for his highly talented task force. They made stabs at it, but it was like trying to eat ice cream with a hot spoon. Jim and his colleagues saw no way out of the maze other than maximum preparedness, while realizing no solution could be perfect. Hence, the early product was not encouraging.

In April, Jim went up to the top floor with his gleanings. "Boss, from what we have now, it looks like economic meltdown worldwide. It'll make nineteen and twenty-nine"—he hated himself for adopting Hodgespeak—"look like a Lego set hit by a blowtorch unless government, banking, finance, and all branches of big business get themselves informed and compliant, starting right now."

Renk's eyes glowed like a banty rooster's. "OK. What I suspected. Worst case: what's the minimum time for compliance in the major economic sectors? Run that for me, then maybe we'll take a little trip."

Jim went back to his computer, networked his task force, and set about making deeper economic forecasts—a job for which he still felt utterly unqualified. As the new on-board academics war-gamed the domino effect of computer system breakdowns in different sectors, the data looked worse and worse: chaos in annuity payments from a major insurance company; halt in production at a transmission component factory in Hamtramck, Michigan; crash of a 300-branch stock brokerage; failure of deliveries from an oil refinery near Los Angeles; a Redball freight train, loaded with perishable fruit and vegetables, stuck on a through line in Nebraska. And then there were foreign impacts on the domestic economy, as well as other considerations: Nuclear energy? Shipment of coal supplies to generating stations? A breakdown in gas supply lines? Disruption of oil supplies from abroad? Reliable electricity? And without electricity, where would we be?

They fed in a few more questionable links, and watched the national erector set tumble. In each test case, the results were far more widespread and ravaging than the initial collapse would indicate. Someone told Jim the British called it the "knock-on effect." He adopted the description.

"Long and short," he told Renk at their next closed-door briefing, "is that wherever you turn, even if one solitary system in a major industry goes down after December thirty-first, ninety-nine, it's going to have an effect we can't begin to calculate. We might be able to if we had a huge dedicated computer of our own. Otherwise, the economy is just too huge, too interconnected."

He went on. "Nationally, it's going to be unpredictable shotgun discomfort. Some disruptions. A lot of inconvenience. Then you start to look at ports here and abroad, and ships. You factor in raw materials—oil, for instance—and finished goods, imports, exports. We suspect the situation gets a whole lot worse."

Renk stared past him, tapping one finger on the desk. "Examples?"

"Oil from Saudi Arabia and Venezuela. Rubber from Brazil. They probably won't even think about remediation till it's too late. Ores we import from Africa, like chrome. Raw materials needed for pharmaceuticals. Other countries? Japan—denial. We're predicting they'll be way behind in getting ready, because face won't allow them to admit to such a major problem. We see a lot of shaky economies going down the tubes, and all of them having an effect here in the US. And if Third World nations suffer any more, they'll blame it on Uncle Sam. That could mean terrorism. In fact, we're already hearing rumbles about biological and chemical weapons, easy to transport and let loose.

"Then there's the possibility that this particular dating sequence is only the beginning of a whole series of snafus in computers—going way, way out in time. But maybe we can leave that to our sons and grandsons."

Renk had his boots on the floor. He rocked in the cowhide chair. "OK. Let's us hit Washington, then Wall Street. None of 'em going to want to hear what we have to say. But I reckon I have enough muscle to get them to listen . . . if we feed 'em a good breakfast. And while you been beavering away, I had some other fellers looking at how we can set up a service operation to help clients debug, get compliant. Only it's gonna cost 'em, and I'm not sure they're gonna want to pay. Nonetheless, that's my worry. Pack your bags and prepare to launch."

"We're doing this for the good of the country, Hodge?"

"I'm as patriotic as the next guy, Jim. More so. But I also believe in the capitalist system, meaning we're doing this for Hodge Renk and his little-bitty girls."

Washington, DC
Spring 1978
Renk pulled every Washington wire he had to get in to see influential senators; committee chairmen in the House; top-level people in the Office of Management and Budget, the White House's watchdog agency; and the General Accounting Office, the congressional equivalent; as well as Treasury and Pentagon officials. Where they could, Renk's Washington lobbying office organized group meetings.

The team from Phoenix spent three hectic days on the Potomac, selling hard—not only the concept of systemic breakdown but also Renk's new service package. Hodge was the quintessential good ole boy: indefatigable, abrasive, brusque, salty, wryly humorous, domineering. He towered in his trademark boots, yet when necessary for impact, he prowled barefoot. Anything to get the attention of his listeners. Jim and a couple of his people provided the flip-chart facts and discussed technical data with their opposites.

Jim slipped away a couple of times to meet some of the contacts he had quietly cultivated. One of them was Dr. Franklin Woodson—"Woody"—a guy who back in the 1960s fought a classic bureaucratic struggle for an innovation he developed that allowed either two- or four-digit dates. He had been outmaneuvered by the Pentagon, which had more computers than any other agency, and which wanted more bang, less useless digits. The hawks of the Potomac won that battle easily while they were losing Vietnam. The young crusaders had actually tried to get private business interested in going to four digits. No soap. The major players were Pentagon contractors, who knew where their bottom line was buttered.

Effective January 1, 1970, the National Bureau of Standards's two-digit date configuration was official policy. Yes, the more foresighted programmers still tried to convince the president to consider the more expensive four-digit alternative. Eventually, they succeeded, but their presentation came across as technobabble, confused and disoriented. The president ended up asking the computer scientist who briefed him if he was able to fix the Nixon family television set.

"And thus," said Jim's confidant over a beer, "the monstrosity you're calling Y2K was born."

Phoenix
Spring 1978
On the way back to Phoenix in the saddle-soaped leather comfort of the family Gulfstream, Renk clinked the ice in his tall glass of Pepsi. "Not a happy camper. Not getting through to them. None of 'em's singing our tune. Knee-jerk rejection," he said to Jim. "They can't see Y2K. Don't want to see it. Won't buy. . . Tell you what. We got a damn good dog-and-pony show going now. We try New York, then LA. If we don't make hay in either of them, we cut our losses, make our own systems compliant, and shut this puppy down. Then we go on to other things that can make some money for Daddy!"

They did just that. After the weekend at home, they set off for New York, where Renk's financial muscle didn't yet outweigh his Arizona brashness. Still, they powered into measured attention on the Street. The breakfasts were lavish, the scrambled eggs warm. But the courtesies were like the rattling of hollow ice cubes. They came up empty again.

Finally, Los Angeles, looking out at the Pacific Rim. But even with the less conventional upstarts of the West Coast, the results were, at best, "We'll get back to you on this."

Everywhere, denial. What they were selling wasn't good for the bottom line. Long-term planning was the next annual report; medium-term was the next quarterly report. Short-term was, "Like, what are we going to do tomorrow, huh?" On the plane home, Renk retreated at warp speed from all-out enthusiasm into the mystery world of the business tycoon. Snarling, he called the operation off. "Gotta know when to fold, is all."

Jim sensed there was more to the announcement. Hodge seemed unusually restrained, even quiet. "Sorry, son . . ."

Jim caught the nuance and was touched. For a moment he felt sorry for his lonely, driven boss, who now mused openly. "Maybe I got too enthusiastic. Maybe I see too far ahead for these folks. Whatever. It don't affect your future with me. I doggone appreciate what you have done. Why don't you take a little vacation down at the villa in Acapulco? And when you come back, we'll figure what you're gonna do from here on out."

Jim nodded, appreciative but wary. He had learned the ways of indirect maneuvering, deviousness, and clandestine mind-set from the Weasel—a name the guys had given Renk long ago—who was a grand master.

Next morning, Saturday, he went into the office and copied as many of his protected files as he could. Jim knew he was skating on thin ice, but he didn't want Hodge's cybergoons usurping or destroying work he still considered vital. Anyway, he rationalized, since the project was a bust, any violation of company security would be of relatively little concern at this point.

* * *

Jim had started to plan even during that flight back from Washington. Last year, he'd run into an ex-Air Force buddy at an electronics expo in Vegas. They reminisced, as old computer warriors do, and compared careers. Bud had advanced farther and quicker in his corporation—Hi-Tech Space Systems (HSS)—than Jim had with Renk. As they exchanged business cards, Bud said, more than casually, "Hey, Jim, if you ever think of leaving that lunatic asylum, call me. Always looking for good men. And we know you. Maybe even better than you're aware of."

The last was delivered with an almost innocent smile. Then Bud was gone before the bumfoozled Jim could ask for clarification.

Several months later, Jim saw him again at a classy restaurant in Phoenix, where apparently both were massaging contacts. Bud waved. Jim acknowledged as subtly as possible. Afterward he wondered if it had been pure coincidence.

Mid-June 1978

Twenty minutes after he had settled back into his desk chair and started to play catch-up, Jim got the summons. While he'd been recharging on the Pacific shores, the mood had changed. He was not invited to sit. Instead, he trailed Renk at a dogtrot to the executive elevator, and then they limo'ed out to Phoenix's Sky Harbor Airport.

As the Gulfstream's engines spooled up with an earsplitting whine, Renk hollered, "I think better out of the office."

They took off, headed south over Mexico, then west over the Sea of Cortez and Baja. Jim lost track as they cruised again over land. He waited, knowing pretty much what was coming.

Hodge Renk was blaming him for the failure of the Y2K Project, pure and simple. "I seen this coming. Knew it was going to tank after Washington, but I let you talk me into those other presentations. You got too big for your britches, boy. Thought you could run this here company I built up from smaller than a piss-ant gopher hole. So now, listen up! When things go cattywampus, you just gotta learn to take your lumps, same as I did, is all. Not push it off onto your superiors or the down-belows. Stand up for what you believe in. Only way to get ahead.

"Why, I bet you had yourself all suited up for one of my high brass suites one of these days, huh?" Renk was nearly spraying. "Maybe even have a little-bitty jet like this for you personally? Did I ever give you any notion you might make out like that?

"No way did I! And you wouldn't make a good husband for either of my little girls, neither. I saw you eyeing my Sharylynne at the barbecue. Maybe gettin' ready to paw her, too! Hell, you're not even from Arizona. Whatever." The workings of the Renk mind were beyond boggling, Jim thought for the umpteenth time.

"You didn't give me enough to go on, is what happened." Renk paused hardly long enough to draw in air to spew his spittle. "I couldn't convince those guys in Washington. Ammunition you gave me was too low-caliber. Hell, some of the time you were feedin' me blanks. Made me look bad." His boots drummed against the metal underpinnings of the table, audible over the jet engines.

"I don't like having them suckers look down their Eastern noses at me. Even if the half of 'em come from out here. Snottier schools, is all." Now he stemmed the mist of vituperative spray, and honked noisily.

"Fact is, you became a liability. Some of the people we talked to—powerful people who like me and trust me—told me you were kind of a troublemaker. Asked me why I kept you. Told 'em I stick by my own people, but I gotta tell you, you didn't make us a whole lot of friends in some places where friends are what I need. People to do a lot of business with.

"Now, put yourself in my boots. One hand, I got a bright young feller full of ideas that rub some people the wrong way, and a lot of 'em are folks who I've got major contracts with. What would you do? I could hang you out to twist!"

Jim kept himself from glancing at the lock on the Gulfstream door.

"Fire you, even." The storm calmed in a split second. "But I'm a reasonable man. My philosophy is, if you can't sell it, it don't exist. Not a starter. Back to square one. Period. Wipe the files clean. Move on."

Jim was surprised at his own calm. He judged Renk's performance coolly: Hodge was better than an overage in-grade captain, but still he lacked something. Credibility? Ability to inspire? A real sense of creativity? He'd never make it higher than lieutenant colonel. Jim knew part of Renk's fury was over the proprietary information in his head which, short of lynching, IEMS could not control.

"Even though you let me down so bad, I still like you. In spite of what you done to me. Yessir! Don't do to hold no grudges, my little-bitty girls tell me. Not Hodge Renk."

He lifted the phone from the armrest and ordered the captain to steer for home. The plane curved gently back over the spine of the Rockies, and headed south over the darkening desert. "So, now," he continued, "I'm gonna make you an offer you better not refuse. You listen good, hear? Old scores forgotten. New start . . . I got a slot for you up in Columbus, Ohio. On the rim of the automobile industry. They're getting seriously into robotics up there. Gonna be a hot spot one of these days."

Jim was again surprised at how relaxed he felt. Was this the guy he damn near thought of as a *father* at one time or the guy he had briefly speculated might push him out the plane door into the mountain vastness? Was he for *real*?

"Columbus?" he finally asked, incredulous.

"Heartland. Good solid people." Renk eyed Jim closely. "No phony Eastern airs to them. No salary reduction. Moving expenses. Good housing, they tell me. Get you out of the limelight for a while.

"You'll chill down from this assignment, get your feet wet in another field. When your performance reports look good again, I'll bring you back down here—maybe a couple of years.

"Of course, you get a bee in your bonnet about talking outta school, I'll remind you—but only once—you signed a secrecy agreement when you came on board. You been handling my proprietary information. It's all mine, everything you did. Don't never forget that! Or I'll come down on you hard as a bucket of horse piss if I need to . . . And I'll tell you this. Some other people just may be watching you to make sure you don't go upsetting any apple carts." Renk paused for emphasis. His weasel eyes seemed almost red in the low glow of the aircraft cabin. "And if they tell me you're a liability," he added, "or you been leaking, I'll dump hard on you. You know that? You oughta."

Then without warning came the softer approach so typical of the mercurial Renk—bitterly angry one minute, paternal but edgy the next. "Someday our time will come, boy. Till then, this is all my stuff, right?"

Hodge Renk finally seemed to have run down, even appeared to deflate in his big leather seat. Jim mused that this driven, insecure, hugely wealthy man had feelings, and that he could sometimes tire just from keeping up the front. Although hard to discern, hidden way down beneath the armor plating, there was a human being. Jim was almost sorry for him, but he seized the opportunity Renk now presented.

"I brought this with me. Figured you'd be saying what you did." He handed over a letter of resignation. "It's been a hell of an experience, Hodge. No hard feelings. Like you'd say if you were in my shoes, 'Time to move on. Put this behind us.'"

Renk squinted across at him. He looked tired, shriveled. "You got more guts to you than I figured. I like that." He cartwheeled Jim's envelope between his fingers and added, without opening it, "OK, I'll give you a good severance settlement so you're not hurting financially. And anytime you want to talk, the door's always open to you. Go on out there and make your fortune. You deserve it. Any idea where you're going?"

"No, not yet. I've had one or two feelers."

"So, been creeping around behind my back? Well, might have expected it. You're a savvy young feller, and all's fair, like they say. Just forget this Y2K shit. It never existed. Figment of imagination. I'll take care of the in-house fellers. The people we talked to outside, hell, they lost interest the minute we walked out of those rooms."

Jim was surprised at Renk's calmness, his calculatedness. He had expected a geyser to erupt at the betrayal, rather than a cool, cut-your-losses dismissal.

Renk grabbed the intercom. "OK, Captain, let's put this sucker down. Gotta get back to my girls. Supper's waitin'."

CHAPTER FOUR

Sedona, Arizona
Late 1970s

Jim fully expected his phone to be tapped, so he drove up to the red-rock splendor of Sedona, rented a motel room, and started working the phone.

He needed some perspective. First on his list was Woody—Dr. Franklin Woodson, the expert on information systems he'd met on his Washington rounds. Woody concealed his sharply analytical and intuitive mind behind a folksy facade, and he enjoyed playing the paradox: a down-home kind of guy who seemed to fit better in the weather-stained swing seat of a ranch-house porch than in a cowhide swivel chair in a carpeted corner suite at the Office of Management and Budget, yet whose mind was tungsten hard and razor sharp.

Woody listened without interruption to what Jim said. Then he replied in the border state drawl he had not allowed Washington to erase, "You be careful, young feller. Sounds to me as if you might have got yourself on a couple of shit lists."

Together they reviewed a slate of the painfully few people in Washington who still worried about the Y2K problem. Jim had transcribed their information to a private file that was now a prize possession.

Woody's soft voice hardened, tinged with warning. "There's still some stuff going on out here—has been ever since the sixties—that's pretty touchy. Some of us fought that two-digit ruling all the way to the top, but we were outpowered. The people responsible for that decision, those guys across the river, they don't want folks nosing around. That's all I can say. Just take care." Woody hung up abruptly.

Jim wiped his brow. His mind made computerlike connections. Someone had Hodge Renk by the curlies. The deduction wasn't rocket science.

He drove out to look at the huge red boulders that made Sedona such a spectacular site. Once again composed, he went back to his room and got through to Janet Montori at Social Security.

She greeted him warmly. "It's been two years, hasn't it, Jim?"

"Going on three."

They chatted like old friends for a couple of minutes. "So," she said then, "is there something I can do for you, Jim? I think I owe you one."

He told her, as briefly and securely as he could, what he had been up to.

Janet's reaction was brisk. "What's it got to do with me? With Social Security?"

"I was just wondering if you've made any headway on Y2K."

"Yes, we have. But not as much as we'd like. Middle management is aware. Topside is scared pissless—if you'll pardon my French—about the political implications. If we can just get them to be gutsy, we're going to try for a special budgetary allocation to fix the Bug. But it won't be easy. There may be tough opposition from . . . Well, let's just say, from within the government. Why are you asking?"

"I've got a job offer that's talking real money," Jim replied, "but I'm also thinking of moving back out West, maybe setting up a private consultancy sometime soon. I'd like to be able to use you as a personal reference. Maybe I could say SSA was first to act on Y2K because I briefed you. Would you be OK with that?"

"Let me think on it." Janet paused. "In principle, sure. You earned it. If you're serious about working Y2K, there's a small core of middle-management people in other agencies who might be interested. It'd have to be very back-channel, of course. The people who have real clout, they want this whole thing to go away. We—you—can't be too careful. Get my drift?"

The Washington syndrome, Jim thought. "Maybe if we all got together," he said, "we could do something, you think?"

"We would have to be way discreet, of course," she said. Then she added, "Not that we'd be doing anything subversive. But still, there are lots of people who might misinterpret whatever they don't control."

Jim recognized the warning. "Yeah, going freelance doesn't make much business sense right now. But in a while, maybe I could make a living at it. And do some good." He could feel the possibilities fading, at least for the time being.

"Good luck, Jim." Genuine warmth returned to her voice. "And please stay in touch. Let me know where you locate. Maybe we can put something together down the line."

Jim tried to relax in his motel room, but his mind churned. He was sure the time would come when he would have to feed the media to get the Y2K message across to the public. Why? Because increasingly he worried about the potential for panic, riots, shooting, looting—worse yet, a major breakdown in society. The message of calm and common sense had to get out where it could counteract hysteria and panic. But this was all speculation, and pretty far out, at that. When it came to the media, Jim Martin was a babe in the woods. He was aware the East Coast corridor people regarded almost anything outside Manhattan and the Beltway with lofty, if not amused, disdain. He wondered if he might be able to take the story to some of the news anchors he respected, like Cronkite, Howard K. Smith or Frank Reynolds at ABC, maybe John Chancellor at NBC.

So what story did he have to sell? Some murmurings about Y2K, an event that *might* take place nearly two decades hence? Even Jim knew that wasn't exactly headline stuff, not in the wind-down after Vietnam and Watergate. Any attempt to create news now would be premature, and would destroy his credibility in the future.

He had watched Hodge Renk manufacture news by creating a gadfly persona and by playing on his bumpkin idiosyncrasies. In public, he was always charging at something others held sacred. Reporters listened because Renk made good copy. Maybe his ideas sounded crazy, but by golly, he *made money*. Jim was a diametric contrast; self-effacing, he was not an ego-driven actor who could match Renk's style. He could never be so outrageous, even if he were desperate to get attention. Hence, first he had to make some money so he could go independent.

Jim grabbed the phone, dialed, and got Bud at HSS. "OK, pardner, let's talk turkey."

Phoenix
October 1979

As Jim prepared to relocate to California and begin his new career with HSS, he wondered often, longingly, about Beth, who had become so much a part of his routine that short eon ago. Here he was racing all the time—hurry-hurry, make careers. He knew he was missing a lot and hoped that in California things might be different.

Sure, there were other girls, casual contacts. Here and there. Jim was also street-smart enough to know that the wives of some of his friends were trying to set him up with this or that girlfriend. He knew, too, that by now he was a pretty good catch, at least if you didn't insist on drop-dead handsome. But always that question intruded, even when he was on the keyboard: *Why am I so nervous?*

Do I really want all this freedom? Where's it getting me? Making money, sure. But face it, this is a pretty dull life. Man ought to think of family, children. Am I frightened of the big commitment? Settling down—with one woman for the rest of my life?

Well, maybe. But would Beth want to—if I got up the courage to ask, or even to phone her again? Now she has a hell of a career going on her own. Pointed at the top of her profession, all right. Would she still be interested in me? A nickel-and-dime engineer with no social graces? We're talking sharing. Money? Hell, got enough, or soon will have. I could make up for what she would lose. Least, I think I could.

Tied down? Hell, I'm tied down now anyway. Might be good to share some of the load. Beth would fit right in. If she were willing even to con-sider it. She always said that when she got settled she wanted to breed horses. What better place? Lots better than the jungles where she can pick up all kinds of diseases—never mind the shots she'd have to get.

Finally, with considerable internal combustion, some hemming and some hawing, Jim got on the phone to Berkeley, only to learn Beth was away on a sample-gathering expedition in Madagascar. Expected back in six weeks, maybe.

Jim noted her ETA on his calendar and called the day after. The same prissily protective secretary said Beth would be busy for the next week, trying to get her office life back together. But yes, she had passed along Mr. Martin's message, and she was sure the professor would return the call as soon as she could.

Jim fretted for the next ten days. This is crazy, he told himself. They had mutually agreed, almost without words, to break off and pursue their separate careers. Yet here he was crawling to her, all but openly admitting he needed her in his life.

Why should she have even thought to wait for him? The parting had been abrupt, just short of angry. Hell, she was attractive, she had a great job. Some creep at the university was sure to have scooped her up in the meantime. But actually there was a chance she *had* been too busy, he said to himself hopefully.

The phone rang, and on the first jingle, he knew it was her. The voice was cool. Not quite indifferent, but reserved. "Yes, Jim. You've been trying to reach me?"

He was stuttering and stumbling. Eventually, after letting him squirm for a few minutes—during which Jim could imagine her smiling—she helped him out. No, she told him in due course, she had not been involved with anyone seriously . . . Oh, a couple of minor flirtations, sure. But she didn't think she really wanted to get involved in a long-distance romance right now. She was very busy, and gaining more recognition by the week.

"Yes, I'd like to see you sometime, Jim. But let's not hurry anything, OK? I've got a lot on my plate; I'm sure you do, too. And frankly, I don't want to travel anywhere for a while." The voice was cool. Jim felt like a trout dazzled by a lure, unable to swim away. Hooked again. But left dangling in the air while the fisher looked for her net.

Vandenberg AFB, California
November 1979

Jim's path was greased. Without missing a beat, HSS assigned him to a high-visibility program at Vandenberg Air Force Base, the United States's West Coast Space Center. And gave him more money than he had reasonably expected from a government contractor.

He quickly found a turn-of-the-century two-bedroom ranch house that needed refurbishing in the Santa Ynez Valley. He figured it had probably served as quarters for a ranch hand on the sprawling Rancho de las Manzanita, back when the Spanish land grants were issued. Divided up over the years, Jim's property was now only a fraction of the old rancho. Manzanita Ranch, as it was now called, extended across 160 acres of oak trees, natural springs, and breathtaking views of the Los Padres National Forest, Lake Cachuma, and Santa Ynez Valley. Jim was awestruck by the beauty of the surrounding land. With his nest secured and his roots firmly planted, he settled in and went to work.

He had responsibility for HSS's share of the Space Shuttle Program. Jim's routine was grinding: two weeks at Vandenberg, then a quick trip to the Kennedy Space Center, or Houston, or a military base where HSS information systems specialists were having problems. Every month, it seemed, he was spending a week in Washington making "house calls" or a couple of days in New York briefing the big wigs at corporate headquarters.

The job designation sounded imposing and dry: Information Resource Management. But it turned out to be an advanced grad-study curriculum in matters that came to be important down the road. He learned more of the ins and outs of dealing with Congress. He also learned, in dismaying detail, that the government wasted huge amounts of time, effort, and money warehousing information. His information management smarts helped shape a program under the Carter Administration that led to passage of the Paperwork Reduction Act in early 1980.

Jim's disks of notes on his activities and contacts, together with a file of private correspondence with some of the officials he had met along the way, now came into play. He sorted out the business cards he had collected, and massaged his contacts around the country.

Was anyone now interested in Y2K? Bottom line: people were polite, but noncommittal. The few hot dogs—those who believed Y2K was a slow-boring termite that threatened the nation—including government nonconformists from Janet Montori's insider list, exchanged information constantly, in keeping with the old 1950s MIT hacker ethic of making knowledge freely available.

With some encouragement from his moles, Jim addressed letters to assistant and deputy secretaries of the major federal departments. Even, occasionally, to a sympathetic cabinet officer. His mail campaign brought only rejections—some couched politely, others brusque—that said, in effect, "Thank you very much for your interest. If that Y2K you talk of becomes a problem, you may rest assured this agency (bureau, department) is well equipped to handle it." Or "Please butt out!"

One morning, Jim watched an analysis spew across his screen from an insider contact in Redmond, Washington: *Here it is again. The Bug warneth and striketh! Like they say in New York, you should live so long!*

He typed his response with furious speed: *Right on, Darth Hummer, but except for us geeks, no one out there believes. Not yet. Not ten years from now. Too damn remote. Can't smell it; can't see it; can't touch it; can't taste it. If people start to believe Y2K exists, they'll think guys like you and me will put the technofix in overnight and everything will be AOK.*

Jim was wound up, feeling a tinge bitter. Then he added: *At least we know it's coming, and when. And when the Great American Public wakes up, people like Renk will make millions out of what we know now.*

His soliloquy to Redmond continued. *So, do we try to corner some share of the remediation market or just try to tell people this is what we are facing, and hope to make enough to get by? I know it's not going to be a hot topic on the lecture circuit, and I won't sign up a whole passel of eager clients. But it's something I gotta do.*

As Jim's outpouring ended, he reflected on his unrelenting idealism scoffed at by so many hardheaded acquaintances. And he wondered, as he had many times before, about the forces that compelled him always to tread a lone path. Nothing in his family background had made him solitary, yet he was happiest when he was working on his own, whether with his brains or with his hands. Revealing his inner world, even to colleagues, had always been difficult. And here, once again, was evidence that he was on his own.

How to go about it? First on his agenda, he had to make money, which would free him up to walk and talk Y2K remediation. Much more important, a decent bank account could help him elevate public awareness—assurance that whatever might come would be a series of inconvenient glitches in the economy but not an insuperable crisis, and was therefore no cause for fear in the years ahead.

So while still with HSS, Jim put himself through a tough twenty-four/seven apprenticeship, working weekend construction jobs. In his few off-hours, he studied for his contractor's license. Once papered, he set up his own building company and began to dabble in real estate as well. He was able to combine the two by building a pleasantly comfortable hotel, the Royal Dansk, in Solvang. By then, Jim knew he had the cushion he needed to work on Y2K. Maybe, he at times admitted to himself with unvarnished patriotism, he could pay back something he and his family owed to this beneficent country.

* * *

Among the people Jim saw in the few hours he was not engaged to his computer, or wielding tools on a building project, was a stunning couple with a shared interest in horseflesh. These two were to play a considerable part in his reformation and social elevation.

Down the Valley road from Los Olivos, Roger Foster lived at a butte-top ranch with a commanding view of the Santa Ynez Valley. Roger was an international seven-goal polo player. His wife, Danielle Johanssen, a former horse show champion, was now a freshman state assemblywoman in Sacramento. That she was a down-the-line Democrat brought considerable mirth to—and a few heated discussions with—her husband, and in time, Jim.

Ever since his early experiences with the streets of Pasadena and the clamor of the Rose Bowl Parade, Jim had yearned to be a horseman, and Roger and Danielle obliged, teaching him the true pleasures of riding. From Roger, he learned to ride Western and to play polo; from gazellelike Danielle, he learned about dressage, jumping, and the hunt. Enchanted, he began to allow more time for riding, without letting his business pursuits slide. Despite the heady excitement of work at the Space Center and in Washington, he was happiest out in the hills overlooking the Santa Ynez Valley while riding Mercury, his calm, sure-footed gelding. And as he rode, he sometimes let his thoughts drift to Beth, up in Berkeley or off in some place he could hardly imagine, swatting mosquitoes and yearning for a good shower and some decent soap.

Jim loved to ride the sparse trails known only to the cognoscenti—up and around Figueroa Mountain and into the Los Padres National Forest. In time, he attained membership in the Santa Ynez Trail Riders, a group of wealthy, powerful, and sophisticated businessmen who every few months took elaborate three-day rides through some of the old rancheros in Santa Barbara county. The organization had its roots in the early history of California's rodeos and roundups. The trail riders fancied themselves modern-day vaqueros, or cowboys, and visited ranch after ranch to assist their hosts in calf branding, steer roping, cattle sorting, and bronc busting. As drawn as he was to the cowboy ways, Jim enjoyed returning from these long weekends to the hot tub, a cold martini, and the eiderdown-filled king-size bed that awaited him at Manzanita Ranch.

Before long, Roger and Danielle had "civilized" Jim, as he often put it, lifting him out of his awkwardness. And now he was knocking on French doors of prosperity and respectability in one of the most desirable and beautiful areas of America. Riding was a natural adjunct to his new life, and perhaps also, he reflected with a smile, a way into circles otherwise denied him.

Thus, while pursuing his two careers, he slipped into a third—that of gentleman cowboy. The stamp of approval had come when Roger first asked him up to the Polo Ranch for lunch. There he knew he was welcome. Soon afterward, Roger asked him over for dinner, with what Jim thought might have been more than his usual casualness. Seated at the big polished table, Danielle steered the conversation around to Jim's personal life.

"You know, you work so damn hard. Two jobs. Night and day. You never relax except when you go out riding with the guys. How about you come down to Palm Desert with us a couple of weekends from now? Roger is playing on a team with Prince Charles."

Jim almost dropped his fork. "Uh . . . do you mean *the* Prince Charles?"

"Yes, *the* Prince Charles! We'd like to have you as our guest. Be good for you—a weekend away from computers, hammers, nails, and spreadsheets."

"Well . . . I was going to reroof the shed, make it into a better office for myself . . ."

Roger broke in. "You can do that the weekend after. There aren't going to be any downpours before then. Come on, it'll be a damn good party."

Jim acquiesced as gracefully as he could. Later, however, he panicked. He hastened down to a men's haberdasher in Santa Barbara to get himself outfitted, renting the finest tux he could find. Then, feeling fairly well prepared to face British royalty, early Friday morning he joined Roger and Danielle to fly down to the desert in their private plane.

The plot unfolded rapidly. As Roger went to check the ponies before a warm-up game, Danielle navigated Jim over to the pavilion, newly refurbished for the prince's visit. Jim got them each a cup of tea and they sat outside in camp chairs, watching the players knock the wooden balls back and forth. Danielle seemed a bit fidgety, a change from her usual warm-but-controlled self.

"Anything wrong?" Jim asked, keeping his mouth open and wondering whether he had put his foot in it.

"Oh no, just unwinding. Let's relax and watch the practice."

Soon, a Lincoln pulled up and parked in a reserved spot next to the pavilion. Danielle lifted her chin to watch the car, Jim noticed, as two people—an elderly man and a younger woman—got out and came toward them. As they drew closer, Danielle smiled. "Some old friends of ours, Jim. Arthur Oldfield and his daughter Beth."

Jim was speechless. Beth was radiant, tanned, smiling. "Hi, Danielle!" she said. "Going to introduce me to your handsome friend here?"

The laughter over the trick the ladies had played was genuine, and even Jim could not keep from joining in at his own expense. In a momentary aside, Danielle said sternly, "You're one very lucky guy, Jim. I don't know why she waited for you, but she did. Now treat her right, damn it!"

That night, after drinks and a sumptuous dinner at the hotel, everyone sat around and played table-stakes gin rummy. Soon enough, Roger, Danielle, and Arthur Oldfield disappeared to catch their zzzs before the next day's royal match. Jim and Beth lingered and talked.

Jim was overwhelmed with gratitude that she'd made the party and its people so easy for him to adapt to. Beth fit in well among the comfortably wealthy. She was on home turf, and she was everything

Jim was not. It was a side of her life she had considered unimportant, and unnecessary to reveal when they were in Berkeley together. Now she filled in the blank spaces.

Her father, a knock-off copy of John Wayne, was a cattleman who owned spreads in Wyoming as well as near Salinas, in Monterey County, the Steinbeck country of Central California. He had sent Beth away to a boarding school outside Phoenix, which specialized in giving well-heeled ranch children poise in English saddles as well as on the ballroom floor. It was there that Beth and Danielle had met and become best friends . . . and schemers for each other's welfare forever after.

There, too, Beth had stunned her father and her friends with her uncommon brainpower, often challenging the faculty. With her soaring interest in biology, then in botany, she had promptly been accepted by the University of California at Berkeley. Jim knew the rest.

Next day, the two sat close as His Royal Highness's team won one and lost one against another team selected from among America's finest high-goal players. The ball that night at the La Quinta Country Club was an occasion women dream of and men experience as exquisite torture. Jim didn't dare take a drink to psych himself for the strange social rite, and found his apprehensions were unnecessary. Beth kept him at ease throughout and even guided him through the dances.

Never before had Jim pursued a woman this seriously. Now he knew he had to pursue in earnest.

Roger and Danielle abetted the chase, not that the course was arduous. They invited Jim to accompany them skiing at Vail, and for polo on New York's Long Island. Sometimes Roger would put his plane down in Oakland or Fresno, and Beth would climb aboard for the trip to that weekend's events.

Jim had never been a flower man, yet every week, regular as the readout on a computer, his long-stem roses arrived at the Oldfield Ranch up near Salinas. Jim had also never been a poetry man. Indeed, he had always regarded writing as a laborious but necessary scholarly chore. In pursuit of Beth, however, Jim wrote poetry, even mailed it.

There came a time when they decided to go off together. A bit tentatively, given their past history. They chose the exclusive Mammoth Mountain Inn in the California High Sierras. Dinner ended in the hot tub. And the hot tub ended when they put on their robes and, without many words, went down the hall, intertwined, to Jim's room. It took them only a few meetings to get back to the full intimacy, the easy good humor, the open, voluptuous lovemaking they had thoroughly enjoyed in earlier days, before each had become so frantically entangled in work and worry.

Thereafter, they were as inseparable as business and other demands allowed. Jim extensively modified his work schedule so that they could spend weekends together. Beth, for her part, had no major field trips ahead; instead, she wanted to concentrate on writing up her findings and attending career-building conferences.

Gradually, sheer enjoyment in and of each other returned, whether on a moonlight sail, at a lobster barbecue, or just lolling around a pool. Those were the times out in the open, when they might be observed by someone else. Occasionally, Beth's ingrained modesty would slip just a bit, and she would make a covert lunge for Jim. More often, it was the other way around, and Jim felt overpowered by his love and his yearning for this woman who so captivated him. Then they would move off from wherever the impulse had found them, to take refuge in each other alone, fully and passionately.

Still, Beth had to catch up on the work she had neglected. His phone bill rocketed. Beth was amused, but didn't tease him. Rather, she was content to let things unfold.

With what seemed to him madly romantic yet indecent haste, Jim decided it was time to make an honest woman of Beth. Actually, he admitted to himself it was he who was not comfortable with the still slightly furtive nature of their meetings and with their intimacy, which to him seemed almost illicit. Maybe, he grinned privately, it was *he* who needed to be made honest!

He laid it all on. They flew to Hawaii, and stayed at a sumptuous hotel on Kauai with views in every direction. On the second evening, Jim led Beth to a spot he had picked, where the hotel staff had set out champagne and caviar. Then as the sun set over the vast Pacific, he asked her to be his wife. Beth's eyes brimmed, and her smile was dazzling. She did not hesitate to accept, whereupon Jim managed to slip on her finger a substantial diamond he had bought in Santa Barbara, without dropping it.

Later, as they looked back on the romance, Jim, still somewhat sheepish, commented to Beth, "I was like a lovesick calf." And she replied, "Yeah, sure. A calf that never let me out of the hotel room!"

They married, fittingly, on an October Saturday in 1981 at Jack and Danielle's ranch overlooking the Santa Ynez Valley. Everyone who was anyone from the Valley, as well as a number of politicos and high rollers from the state and even national scenes, was there. People Jim knew by name or by sight who were cheek-kissing friends of the Oldfields. The bride wore a traditional long gown; the groom felt awkward in a cutaway, but was supported by Roger, his best man, and by the presence of his own father, up from retirement in Pasadena, and his mother.

Roger and Danielle had tried to insist it was their party, but the bride's family stole the home advantage and, after some friendly jostling, managed the affair. The bride was chauffeured to the large marquee by her father, in a carriage pulled by a matching pair of dapple-gray geldings. The tent for the reception was huge, and in it a dance floor had been laid. The catered buffet ran the gamut from smoked sturgeon and caviar to a spit-roasted steer and baked alaska. A ten-piece band, which had appeared on national television and in one movie, entertained in every style known to *Billboard*.

Exhausted, exhilarated, and supremely happy, the newlyweds settled into the now rechristened and refurbished Manzanita Ranch.

* * *

Beth gave birth to Kate at the local hospital on a golden fall morning in 1982. During the final months of Beth's pregnancy, Jim had moved, with some apprehension, into the new realm of fatherhood. Until now, tending to a woman as she headed toward giving birth, watching her miraculous changes, and anticipating the arrival of his child had seemed a shadowy, even unlikely, event far away in his future. With tiny Kate in his arms, however, the future had unexpectedly become the present. Henceforth, he realized, he would be responsible for both Beth and Kate, their provider and guardian—for life. And while this new responsibility carried more weight than he had imagined, it also awakened a new self-awareness. To his pleasant surprise he felt even more of a man. Too, he discovered a new dimension to his love for Beth, a new sensitivity to their union.

Now two had become three. Jim's vision of the rest of his life, previously so solitudinous, was irrevocably altered. Best of all, he felt stabilized. And happy.

One late afternoon in August, the outdoors beckoned irresistibly. Beth and Jim saddled up their horses. Jim buckled on the papoose frame he liked to wear, and Beth gently slipped Kate into it while she was still asleep. They rode out of the corral and up a faint bridal path that wound through gnarled California oaks, then onto the crest of a hill overlooking the Valley. The faded stubble of vineyards had yielded to lush greens of Chardonnay and Pinot Noir vines, climbing in carefully tended rows up the slopes of a subsidiary canyon. Below, contented cattle ambled toward their barn, in no hurry to desert the glow of the outdoors.

"It's almost like a Grandma Moses," Beth mused. "So idyllic. So quaint in this day and age. Jim, we're very lucky, very blessed. Sometimes I think we're protected—by God, I guess." Her words, although genuine, came out awkwardly.

"Yeah," Jim responded. "I want to take Kate out and hold her up, and say, 'Hey, little girl. This is it! It's worth the struggle. To live here and preserve this place. To protect what we're seeing and feeling.' One day she'll understand. And she'll love it like we do. We've just got to get through the next twenty years happy and prosperous—for her."

Beth smiled. "You know, you really are almost a poet when you get wound up. You ought to talk like that more often." Jim was embarrassed, and just a little misty-eyed.

The trio continued, the two horses picking their way among rocks and roots in the lazy mood of the pastel dusk, and pausing occasionally for a mouthful of grass. As the sun began to slip behind a high western ridge, the riders headed for home.

That evening, after a quick dinner of leftovers, and the usual reading out loud, which they believed in, they snuggled Kate down, then returned to the kitchen, where a sheaf of printouts lay neatly ordered.

Beth led off. "OK, where are we going?"

"Part of it's straightforward. The consulting business is growing like gangbusters. I want to keep it that way. Not so much that I have to be gone a lot, but enough to keep our bottom line respectable." Jim looked up, waved a hand defensively. "I'm going to see whether I can still rouse any interest in Y2K. Maybe get some new clients who want to be up to speed on it.

"But I promise you here and now, if I don't make any headway in six months, I'll call it quits and stick to the boring straight-arrow consulting and the property-building-investment business. OK? Deal?"

"And me?"

"What do you want to do, sugar? It's all there. Take your pick."

"First of all, to be a mom. You know, I really don't miss the academic world, as I thought I would. To tell you the truth, I was scared to break away so completely from Berkeley. I guess it was like a womb I had made for myself. For a while there, I thought of the move as entering *your* womb and forsaking my own. I guess I was kind of bitchy at first, wasn't I?" Beth didn't wait for an answer before continuing. "Does this make sense to you?"

Jim nodded, puzzled but attentive.

"I don't miss the travel, and the mucking about looking for new plants, or talking to indigenous people. Oh sure, I get a bit antsy, but the transition has been a lot easier than I expected. And now, my life's here. I can keep up with developments on the Internet . . . But you know, I'm not even doing *that* anymore. So, to answer your question, I won't take time away from Kate, but I really want to start breeding the horses as soon as I can. It'll be a business, too. I know it will."

"That's a pretty big set of operations for us, isn't it?"

Beth frowned.

"OK, I'll back off." Jim shifted gears. "We can do all of it—I know we can. And still live in the best place in the world." He was mind-spinning, something he loved to do. "Maybe, in a while, a little brother for Kate? Want to do a garden too? Start thinking about self-sufficiency?"

"Maybe, but let's not go into overdrive. I think something big is happening for sure. And we need to approach it cautiously, one step at a time."

Jim grinned and happily yielded to his wife, as he so often did.

Time went by like a pack of flash cards.

After more than a decade of advising public and private organizations on managing their information resources and technology, Jim had felt it was low-risk to go out on his own. By mid-1983, he had more work than he could handle. But he didn't want to take on employees, so he referred a great deal of the work to his amazed competitors. He was, he explained, "happy to be sittin' in the catbird seat," as Red Barber, a legendary old baseball broadcaster, used to say.

Beth queried this attitude toward business.

"Hell, honey," he replied. "I figure if I start making too much I'll get greedy. Then the things and the money will become more important than the kind of life we have here. We have more than enough to live on. Anything you think we need? You can drive only one car at a time. Eat one meal. Watch one TV. Want to go on a vacation? Say where and we're gone—provided we can fix things up for Kate. To be honest, it gives me a kick to say no when I don't want to deal with some guy."

"Wouldn't you know I had to go and marry the world's most rational man. And I'm glad I did."

Every once in a while, he wondered out loud if Beth felt left out by all his computer, consulting, and construction activity.

"Sometimes I get a bit resentful," she admitted one evening, "but it doesn't last long. It's not like I sacrificed to put you through grad school—something a lot of other women did for their men. Instead, I figure I got more than I gave. It took me time to realize that. Sure, I was restless at first, and you noticed but didn't comment on it. Now the horses take up all the time I want to spend away from Kate and you. And I'm making some headway."

She paused and smiled. "You know, we're going to sell that mare for good money and a reasonable profit. OK, it's not food for the mind, but it does bring satisfaction." Beth beamed an engulfing smile as she came into Jim's arms. "I wouldn't change this life for anything."

Shortly after Kate's first birthday, the Reagan administration had appointed Jim a member of the White House Conference on Productivity, where he was named vice-chair of a subcommittee, along with his friend Woody. After two years of coast-to-coast meetings and conferences, the committee delivered farsighted recommendations to be implemented during the rest of the Gipper's tenure. The recommendations were rooted in Jim and Woody's overriding belief that knowledge and information are valuable capital assets—and indeed, knowledge was soon to become one of America's major exports. Adapting the committee's technospeak to management terms, Jim's team suggested: "Private sector organizations should recognize the strategic role of information and information resources on productivity and profitability. They would do well to develop information strategies in conjunction with product development, marketing, financial, and management strategies. In short, the private sector should treat information as a strategic asset; tie information to strategic planning; and raise the responsibility for information resources to top levels of the corporate structure."

After the report, Jim again surveyed his landscape. He was restless. He was in demand, especially in Washington, as a world-class information systems expert, making six figures, but with no profit-sharing options in HSS. Six days of independent consulting would provide the same income as a month's work for HSS.

The corporation had become, if not a strait jacket, at least a restrictive harness on his abilities. It was, once again, time for a move.

Jim knew that all government agencies routinely sent people to cutting-edge conferences to stay up to speed on developments in their sectors. On the social fringes of these gabfests, Jim massaged contacts and built his network. Treasury, Interior, Agriculture—in time, all asked him to consult. He quietly hoped the Defense Department which, apart from the National Security Agency and CIA, had the most advanced supercomputers in the world, and would one day take notice of him. But he got no nibbles from the classified establishment.

He began to slip into the bind he had dreaded. Some of the work required him to spend time in draining cross-country travel, depriving him of "our time," as he and Beth referred to it, at Manzanita Ranch. Sometimes, too, when he glanced at the calendar, he reminded himself that the years were slipping away; the nation was ticking closer and closer to year 2000. Now, at Thanksgiving 1986, the country was basking in the glow of prosperity under Ronald and Nancy Reagan.

With Kate tucked away one evening, Beth made a glass of yellow zinger iced tea for herself, and for Jim a "Nordy"—his favorite iced-tea-and-lemonade mix. (The name for the concoction was a private joke: if Beth binged at all, it was to mount an occasional one-woman raid on Nordstrom's, the upscale department store in Santa Barbara, for which Jim teased her mercilessly. She, in turn, hit upon Nordy as an appropriate name for Jim's drink of compulsion.) They then sat down to a family council.

"OK, you're doing too much," Beth began bluntly. "I see you too little. Kate needs you here. You've got more work than you can handle. Can you cut back and still earn enough to keep us afloat till the horses start bringing in some real money?"

"I think so. Maybe I can offload one or two of the clients onto someone else. Otherwise, my rap sheet's pretty good. I can jack up my prices, and I'm almost sure folks will pay."

Beth looked deep into his eyes. "And what about your Y2K Bug?"

"Well, I'll tell you." Jim grinned his cookie-jar smile. "I've been talking to some of the guys, mostly Treasury, OMB, GAO, Department of Ag, HUD, Social Security, as well as congressional staffers, even civilians. We have a kind of loyalist underground network that goes back years, often to the service. We exchange updates so we're all on the same page. But we—especially the guys who're still in harness—have to be very secure. Everyone suspects a major flap's coming, because people in the power structure are so shortsighted, or power mad, or greedy. When any of them talks to the front office, it's same old 'Forget it. You're dead meat if you keep on plugging this Y2K stuff.'"

He paused, with a look of discouragement. "If anyone gets too obvious, they're hung out to dry by the Pentagon. Defense, which decided way back there is no Y2K, has its ways of stomping out dissenters. If you're in the ranks, of course, you're no problem: all they do is hint at an assignment of polishing latrines in Alaska or Turkey, and you fall into line. Civilian employees, they can transfer to a bookkeeping slot on some island. Guys who work for defense contractors, the old-boy net takes care of. People like me, they just brownlist."

Jim paused again, then went on. "I gotta say, I wonder if the real reason Renk dumped me so fast was pressure from the Pentagon. Maybe I really *did* become a liability, as he once said. Wouldn't surprise me—he's always had a lot of military contracts. But that's no nevermind. The work keeps rolling in here, whether or not the military-industrial establishment thinks I'm dangerous.

"Some of the guys I know," he went on, "are so burned out trying to convince senior management, they're quitting as soon as they've served their twenty. No way do they want to be anywhere nearby when year two thousand hits the fan. They know they'd be blamed for not warning the boss-class in time, so they're setting up as consultants, like me. Some of them just get cushy private sector jobs and lay low. But soon as Y2K comes out of the closet, soon as people realize what's going to hit us, we'll all be swamped with work, and the rate for consultants will be astronomical. Just wait!"

"What about your clients? They listen to you, don't they?"

"When it comes to info systems, yes. On Y2K, they freeze. Sometimes a tech guy will say, 'We can't possibly slip an allocation into next year's budget to fix something that won't happen for more than ten years. The bean counters would think we're nuts. No dice.' It's too remote. They look at me like I'm a leftover from Haight-Ashbury. And I know where they're coming from. So we'd better give it a rest. The time will come."

Beth looked at her husband lovingly. "Till then?" she asked quietly.

"Thanks for not pushing me too hard. Letting me see the truth for myself. As of tonight, I'm . . . out of the Y2K business. I'll still talk to the guys, keep in touch. But I won't try to sell the idea anymore. For now. You OK with that?"

Beth smiled and came to him. "Deep in my heart, I know you're right about Y2K. Really I do."

"*I* know I'm right, too. And it's not an easy one to let go of. We'll see . . ."

Beth and Jim watched the Reagan supremacy and the roll of the good times, the ascendancy of the boomers and their awesome preoccupation with trendy material goods. They felt no envy that they were missing all the yuppie one-acters in the happening places. Then in the recession of the late 1980s, Jim's income dipped. But the investments they had made, plus business that still came in, kept their heads well above water. Nor did real estate and construction stop completely.

"Any way you look at it," Jim said to Beth, "we're still a lot better off than those people in the big corporations being pink-slipped right and left. People losing their houses. Foreclosures on farms. The old American Dream looks a bit shaky, maybe?"

Kate grew; Beth observed. Full of wonder, hating the discipline she occasionally had to mete out, she loved every moment of her daughter's being. Evenings when Jim was traveling and Kate was bedded down, Beth turned off the lights and let the beauty of her surroundings sweep over her. In these moments she came upon expansive ideas that made sense, if only to her.

Beth had always read far more than her friends. Serious stuff. In the 1970s, as the environmental movement got rolling, she absorbed the Club of Rome's *Limits to Growth* and its successor, *Mankind at the Turning Point*. From them she derived her firm belief that the world was facing the *problematique,* or linkage of the major challenges facing humankind—land use, exploitation of capital, global pollution, population growth, dwindling natural resources, war and terrorism, on and on. She knew the methodology of the two studies had been flawed, but she held firm to the conviction that what the Club's scientists had said was basic truth, and a stern warning to all.

Now, a new knowing overtook her. She thought of her husband, unashamedly convinced that Y2K was a serious challenge to society. No, she realized, it wasn't really about Y2K. The Millennium Bug was a symptom of something more far-reaching—a shift in the way people looked at things.

She knew some of the deep thinkers of the time were speculating about a global transformation. Sometimes when Jim was away, she'd delved into David Bohm, Fritjof Capra, Rupert Sheldrake, Peter Russell, Ralph Abrams, and other modern-day scientist-philosophers who pushed the boundaries of science into metaphysical, even spiritual realms, and who had startling answers to age-old questions. Maybe, she mused, Y2K was the trigger for what they were talking about. Maybe, too, she reflected, it would not be such a bad thing, considering what the present template had brought.

Would there be a significant change in the way things worked? A shakeup in social and political institutions, some of which were already visibly crumbling? Everywhere you looked, things weren't going as they might be. Sure, the materialism insulated people handily from the inner sense of unease many felt, when they allowed themselves to feel at all. Anything, in those endlessly multiple leagues, was better than true self-examination. But people's overriding emphasis on *things*—the complacent conviction that possessions were the sole protection against uncertainty, the sole index to status, even worthiness—wasn't the spirit in which America was built.

There was a nastiness to the times, Beth thought. A lack of scruples—a word she didn't hear much anymore. An edginess. Cutthroat divisiveness. Devil-take-the-hindmost competitiveness. All of it for purely material rewards. Where was satisfaction in work? Was honesty only for the weak, the disenfranchised? Was the game no longer about what you produced but about how nimble you were, how sycophantic you could be? Who dared to plunge their hands into the earth, get them callused and dirty, and watch life grow? There was so little reliance on solid accomplishment now that humanity was moving farther and farther away from nature.

Global warming? Presently it concerned not just academic circles (she could not bring herself to think of the jousting egos and petty politics of academe as a "community") but also populations, through the scourge of uncontainable disease as well as the scarcity of fresh water and the continued plundering of natural resources. The loss of millions of tons of topsoil every year, while the earth turned more dustily friable under the seeding of the petrochemical fertilizers needed to feed billions. The application of capital to projects designed purely to benefit the few. On and on . . . Amid all the waste, indifference, and self-aggrandizing hovered the specter of the have-nots rising in religiously righteous fury that they had been so long denied, launching biological or chemical warfare against First World populations, especially "Satan's people."

Something, it seemed to Beth during these mental excursions, was deeply wrong. Was this, perhaps, why Y2K was positioned to erupt? Was Y2K in fact curable or was it part of a string of events that would bring major change to human lives? Was this what Jim was really dealing with, perhaps without knowing the broader and deeper aspects of the problem with which he was so familiar? For all his love and devotion to family, as well as his humility, Jim was not admittedly religious. Yet his way of doing things was spiritual to the nth.

Beth came out of these periodic reveries at peace with herself and the world, because she knew. She accepted. She had no fear, and had long ago abandoned worry. Which did not mean that she resigned herself to an inevitable doomsday, but rather that she would do what she could with the resources available to her. Her strongest resource was her deep personal faith, backed by a finely honed, well-tempered intellect, and her globe-trotting experiences in the cause of science, with which she could quietly back up, even guide, Jim in his passionate desire to help the world by reducing the long-term effects of Y2K to manageable proportions. When the time was right.

CHAPTER FIVE

Highway 101
July 3, 1990

The driver of an eighteen-wheel juggernaut was cruising back to Los Angeles. More than thirteen hours on the job could lose him his license if he were stopped by the California Highway Patrol (CHP).

He had started with a full load of holiday specials at 4:00 that morning from his company's sprawling depot in the dust grid of East LA; made deliveries along his circuit from Buellton west to Lompoc, north to Santa Maria, on to San Luis Obispo and Atascadero; then headed home. Now, as twilight settled, he was weary, and his rig was nearly empty except for some cardboard for recycling, plastic crates, and shipping bins. He dozed off moments before he was to pass through a level rural intersection—a danger spot he had navigated without worry hundreds of times.

Beth Martin's Cherokee was just picking up speed as she merged onto the interstate from Highway 154. She was running late, trying to squeeze in some last-minute holiday shopping at the nearest major upscale supermarket.

As the driver's hands relaxed on the truck's wheel, the hitch slewed across the freeway. Beth never had a chance. She was killed, probably on impact, which may have been a blessing since the SUV was mangled beyond recognition.

The truck driver was thrown clear of the cab. Although he had not been wearing his restraining belt, and his windows were wide open, he escaped with only a broken arm and scratches. Traffic was blocked for hours.

The CHP later said one of the reasons the driver's eyes might have closed was that the blinking yellow warning light at the turnoff had malfunctioned. The report showed he had a very small amount of alcohol in his system, perhaps one beer, ingested earlier in the day. He was charged with vehicular manslaughter. His license was suspended because of the number of hours he had been working, as was recorded in the logbook. The driver had a wife and five kids in Lancaster, California.

In that instant, Jim's world was smashed into iotas of meaninglessness. After he got over the denial, he alternated between deep sorrow and a desire for revenge. Then he bottomed out; he even talked to Sheriff Mike to see if *he* could do anything to lighten the load the truck driver would carry for the rest of his life. When the case came to trial, the driver was given the minimum sentence; his company drew a stiff fine.

Every now and then, Jim yielded to searching reflection: How could it have happened? Was there significance in Beth's passing? And then he'd succumb to yet another siege of agonized grieving. When days of survivor's guilt had passed, the hollowness was still there. Sometimes as a thought jelled into words, he would turn to open a discussion with his partner and lover, only to remember she was no longer there. He felt as if a major part of him had been suddenly amputated, and it was excruciating, like phantom-limb syndrome— muscle aches that nothing can cure. Jim had never thought he would have to endure such pain.

For a while, nothing got him going, not even riding horses with

Kate, or the earlier pleasure of working with his hands. It took the healing powers of the outdoors, together with a surprisingly competent psychotherapist whom friends had finally persuaded him to see, and the love and support of his amazingly resilient young daughter, for Jim to right himself enough to face the world again.

Ever so slowly, he began to turn the corner back to wholeness again. And during his rehabilitation, Jim learned to allow himself downtime—periods when he would force himself to do nothing but sit, concentrating on a point of light or an object, dissipating his everyday thoughts and allowing his subconscious mind to take over. He soon came to feel that Beth, in her absence, was able to prod him even more than she had in life. Was it real? Could he truly hear her voice guiding him? When he came out of his meditative time, he felt almost embarrassed. It seemed pretty New Agey, and was nothing he could talk about with his friends. Sheriff Mike would for sure never understand. But something was undeniably there, something that approached a physical presence. That much he knew.

Henceforth, in the way of those who suffer irremediable loss, Jim and Kate Martin celebrated the Fourth of July anniversary in their own, very private way.

Santa Ynez Valley
Fall 1993
Three years after the accident, when Kate was eleven, Jim decided he had rusticated enough. All around him were signs that the economy was picking up and, more important, that information highway traffic was roaring by. Jim needed to be out there, high-gearing in the mainstream.

He picked up the traces of his consultancy, worked the phones and the Internet, and was delighted to find he was still highly esteemed by those who knew his work. As word got around that he was back online and available, demand for his services escalated until it was almost unmanageable. Some of the most promising inquiries came from guys he had tossed work to a few years earlier. Jim was pleasantly surprised that Y2K had become more of a byword in technoindustrial circles.

Some savvy corporations were even running pilot programs to see how deeply they might be affected.

He made a comforting arrangement with the wife of a childless couple on the adjoining ranch to care for Kate when he was away. Then he plunged back into the high-tension task of advising on Y2K preparedness and remediation. And by his side, he knew, was Beth.

As the years sped by, Jim prospered, and kept his travels to a minimum. He also found he enjoyed doing homework with Kate, although English and geography were challenges, as they had been decades earlier.

October 1997

Jim stomped into the kitchen, sending eddies of dust motes swirling into the rays of sun lazing on the wooden floor. He had never learned to walk lightly.

"Hey!" admonished Kate, who was trying hard to digest American history. The office phone rang and she grabbed it, answered formally, and—wide-eyed and speechless—passed it to her father.

"Yeah, this is Jim." As he listened, he seemed to gather himself to full height, and then some. "Yessir, that would be me. Back in seventy-seven, seventy-eight? Didn't know you people kept paper that long. Where'd you find them?" He listened intently.

"Well, I'll be damned!" He listened some more as the voice on the phone crackled. "Sure, if I can get a seat, I'll be there! Give me a number and I'll call you back."

Jim was caught between feeling awe and sweating bullets. He grunted something in acknowledgment, hung up, and sat down in a heap. He stared at Kate, who was bursting with curiosity.

He breathed out. "That was the White House."

"I *know*, Dad! I answered, remember? It really was the White House, huh?"

"I'll call back to make sure it's not a hoax, but it doesn't sound like one. They say they found some memos I wrote about Y2K back when I was with Hodge Renk. The people in the President's Council on Y2K want to talk to me, like yesterday."

"My dad and the *president of the United States?* Awesome!" Kate barely restrained herself from scrambling for the phone. "I mean, is this, like serious?"

"We'll know pretty soon, sweetheart. But I don't think I'll be seeing the president. Not this trip, anyway."

Washington, DC
November 1997

Jim was escorted into a crowded, paper-piled office in the Old Executive Office Building, where he was closely questioned on his knowledge of Y2K by a man roughly his own age and a couple of young hotshots—one a politically correct female, the other an ethnically correct male—about his experiences with Renk and the reactions of government officials they had met at the time. All three were friendly enough, but something off-screen made Jim edgy. Were they, perhaps, from the FBI? Investigating, just in case it all hit the fan and the present occupant of the White House needed scapegoats? Or were his antennae spinning too fast, as in the days of Renk-inspired paranoia?

"Understand, we're not on a witch hunt," the senior of the trio assured him smoothly. "And we want to keep Y2K out of partisan politics. We're just trying to get an estimate of where we stand. Off the record, it doesn't look good. We have a lot of work ahead. And yes, to answer the question you want to ask, we are trying to find out, as well, why no one acted back then. Anyway, it's past history. We just want to know who the players are, and were. Quite obviously, we cannot question Mr. Renk himself—it would not be appropriate politically, you understand."

He prepared to draw the meeting to a close. "You've been most helpful, Mr. Martin. Thank you for your time. Of course, we'll reimburse you for the trip."

"Thanks, but no," replied Jim, shelving his misgivings for the moment. "I'm not noble, but I'm OK financially, and the fact that you guys are finally getting ready to act is enough. I hope you'll call me if there's anything I can do to help."

"Oh, we'll be in touch, Mr. Martin. You can be sure of that."

Immediately following the interview, Jim taxied out Connecticut Avenue to visit Woody, his old friend and quasi mentor who, although long retired from the Office of Management and Budget, kept well plugged into the Washington circuitry. Woody welcomed Jim to the familiar, musty, 1930s apartment, wearing the slippers, corduroys, and knit vest that for decades had been his office uniform.

The good public servant peered over his octagonal lenses. "Of course," he began, "nothing has changed. Even if they started remediating today, they wouldn't have enough time to test and check out all the systems." He went on to say that many civil servants he knew—even the chief information officers at some private sector companies who informally called themselves "Woody's Boys"—were choosing to quit now, well before the century flipped over.

"Leaving the sinking ships? Sure. They're scared," he continued. "They don't want to be blamed for what's going to happen, as they sure as hell will be. Even I could go back if I wanted. They offered me a mint. But I'd rather sit here on the sidelines and watch it all play out."

Woody took a sip of his famous sarsaparilla, made from real sarsaparilla root and bark, and smacked his lips. Jim settled back, knowing he was about to be treated to a monologue.

"Of course, the Pentagon knows it made a god-awful mistake back then. Back-channel word is, the brass are spending damn near as much time covering their asses as they are on remediation. In a way, you got to feel sorry for them over there, even if they brought it on themselves, and the country.

"Oh, GAO will do an investigation and sort of point the finger at the military. And then Congress will hold some sad-ass hearings, but it'll be the usual whitewash for the record—one of those things that just happens and is then filed away with a gazillion other documents that will soon enough decay and disappear into dust. Even after base closings, there are still plenty of senators and representatives beholden to the sovereign state of Pentagon.

"Of course, my son and I have our plans all set. You can bet we won't be in Washington! This city is going to be a disaster, thanks to that mayor we had . . . No sir, we've been upgrading our cabin out in West Virginia so we'll be able to handle anything that comes—short of warfare. But I do draw the line at guns."

Jim thought he detected a pause, and jumped in. "What's your take on this White House office I was in? I felt like they were giving me a grilling."

Woody shrugged. "I hear those people are trying to do as good a job as they can. But no money. Not enough staff. No clout. Basically, an advisory committee . . . I hear they're going to announce real soon they're bringing a guy over from OMB who has a rep as a pretty cool crisis-manager. Does poker face real well. They'll send him out on the circuit to talk calm but also give everyone a submessage that they're on their own. The feds will have their hands full, and they know it. When this thing goes big, all hell will break loose, and no one wants to be held accountable, certainly not this president. Or the vice president. So it's almost dead certain Y2K is going to be a political matter . . . 'Yeah, right,' as my grandson says. No way it couldn't be.

"If I could give you a bit of advice, young man, I'd suggest you cozy up to that Senator Ezra Palmer, the one who heads the Senate subcommittee on Y2K. He's doing a pretty savvy job. I reckon you'll make more headway with him than with the people down at sixteen hundred. Can't do much without a leader, and ours is either out on the golf course or raising money, or thinking about his niche in history, or still busy cleaning up the record.

"You want to get involved, you go up to the Hill for your slice of the action. More than that, get your people at home organized. Make damn sure they're prepared! Now, vamoose. I need a nap."

Before booting him out, Woody helped Jim locate Janet Montori, whom he'd lost track of in his isolation. Back at the hotel, Jim was pleased to hear her voice on the first try. Janet, now deputy director of

Social Security, told him she had finally gotten money into the budget to go after Y2K. Her team had been working on compliance since 1989. Now they were almost there. SSA was one of the very few federal agencies that would be completely ready. Whether other agencies, like that singular office over in the Treasury that wrote the government's checks, would be up to speed by January 1, 2000—well, that was a different question.

Janet concluded the chat with encouraging words. "I'll send you a write-up we're pretty proud of. And good luck to you, Jim. Stay in touch."

Jim got the fax as he was checking out of the hotel. It was a reprint from one of the specialized online Y2K news services that had recently sprung up:

Social Security Likely to Make It

This is virtually the only Y2K-compliance claim we believe. Social Security is going to make the deadline, no kidding. Why is that?

They've spent a decade (employing over 700 programmers) to fix the Bug. And they'll be done in June of 1999. Aside from the programmers, over 2,800 people worked on the problem. This is exactly why the claims from other agencies that started much later—like the FAA—are simply lacking all credibility. Do the math here: 700 programmers x 10 years = 1,750,000 person-days of work. That's 14 million hours of work, and it doesn't even count the 2,800 nonprogrammers.

So Social Security has spent 14 million hours correcting this problem, according to its own statement. Take any other agency as a contrast. To equal 14 million hours in just two years (because they really weren't seriously working on it until late 1997), they would need to employ 3,500 full-time programmers! If these projects could really be completed in two years, why wasn't Social Security done in 1991?

That's the question to ask. Why does it take ten years to complete the job?

Jim shuttled directly from Washington to New York to meet an emerging figure in the Y2K mix, Dr. Frank Olson—a global economist who worked for a Wall Street powerhouse. Dr. Olson's job was to survey the global economy and report on anything that would have an impact on the billion of dollars his firm and its clients had invested around the world. It was while conducting a survey that he had first become aware of Y2K. He was quick to add it to his highly influential Web page, and thus disseminate his findings to a ready-made blue chip audience in finance, business, industry, and government.

During their brief conference, Olson bluntly told Jim that the more he found out about Y2K, the more concerned he was. But unfortunately, Y2K simply turned his top-drawer readers off. If government and business didn't start taking a more serious approach to fixing the problem, he feared it could plunge the world into a recession. Olson had heard the rumblings that the White House was thinking of some kind of program, but he doubted the administration would make a politically risky move—such as sounding anything more than a muted alarm, quickly followed by reassurance that Uncle Sam was on top of everything.

Jim proffered a thought that had been crystallizing in his mind. "The media can turn a bad situation into panic. They could flip the market over into real chaos, am I right? And that could barrel a recession into a depression, like the crash of twenty-nine."

Olson explained that there were so many uncertainties, so many complexities in what the nation and the world faced, no one could make a bet. As of then, he added, the Wall Street sachem was internally claiming a "high probability" that Y2K would cause a global recession—abetted, of course, by a media establishment that thrived on panic.

Back home, Jim took stock. For once, he was downright discouraged. January 1998 was coming up, leaving less than two years till M-Minute. He'd thought he was being called back to Washington to help in a national confrontation with Y2K, but the short trip had shown him the feds were playing cozy on the problem. It still was an insiders' game.

Y2K was too big to be made into a purely government deal. Maybe he could supplement what the feds were doing. Maybe he could get together with others to cover government's blind side—the public. Or maybe he would simply spend his time alerting people, helping communities prepare for what could be a severe jolt to the American way of life. Perhaps his most important role lay in his own Valley, trying to persuade people to prepare for whatever might come, so they would feel assured they had done all they could in advance.

This was one of the increasingly frequent times in which he sorely wished Beth were at his side to counsel him. But it certainly felt right to try to explain to his neighbors what might happen, and to urge them to get ready. And of course, he still needed to make money. In any case, he knew he'd have to let the real estate and construction business slide.

At times like this, Jim needed something more than his own left-brained way of thinking could give him. He stretched his entire length in the office lounger and yielded to searching reflection. It wasn't another siege of agonized recall; that was now blessedly past. But in his grieving, he had learned to ease himself almost into another world, where he saw things more clearly. Damned if he knew where it came from, but it sure helped.

Now he relaxed fully; took deep, frame-stretching breaths; and let go into the new-but-familiar exhilarating sparkles that tingled through his being, lifting his train of thought out of the chair's womb. Then suddenly he knew why it was so difficult to downplay his intense love for the Santa Ynez Valley. Because it was Beth, nearly personified. A legacy, in far more than goods and land and buildings, to pass on to Kate.

Jim's frame sagged in the lounger. He felt . . . What did he feel—energized? Kind of an airy-fairy word. Rather, comforting. It was truly as if Beth were there with him, inside him, all around him, comforting, encouraging, challenging, provoking.

He delved deeper. "What if . . ."

The answer was there, dangling, elusive but flickering, as if fuzzily etched on a copper plate, or spelled out in subtle back-lit calligraphy. Not harsh. Gossamer wisps. Not crisp, like his mind usually worked. No words loomed out of his mental chasms. It was just there. *Understanding.*

An invigorating flood of warmth passed through, like the lapping of waves on tropical shores . . . only these waves were inside, unseen yet felt. He knew he wouldn't dare define—much less question—their source.

It was as if Beth were saying to him, "*You've mourned enough, and now it's time to emerge from this refuge, to get weaving.*" That phrase. It was one of Beth's favorites, picked up from the English polo crowd.

"*We have things to do—together! Just accept. Incorporate it into yourself.*"

The sense of Beth's presence gave way to an elusive new streaming. Jim struggled to restrain his left brain from trying to calculate the dimensions of the knowing. He risked an unspoken question: "Where to start?"

"*Right here at home, and work out from there. Go with the flow.*"

Jim could only feel, not comprehend, the elation and the bursting from within that overtook him. Not constant; no formula. Sometimes strong, sometimes more subtle. Gentle. Pausing, giving him time to absorb.

The elation brought with it tears of thanks. Jim remembered some New Ager telling him, "Tears are liquid love." Then he accepted the forceful but loving womanly message: "*Surrender! Move on.*" And the not-so-nurturing command, "*Time to get your ass in gear!*"

Jim Martin came out of his meditation quite abruptly, grinning. He had been given his course, and now all he had to do was chart and follow it. Simple.

Santa Ynez Valley
Winter 1977–1998

Come winter, Santa Ynez was spectacular, registering more rain than it had received since records started in the 1880s. When the sun finally came out, the Valley blossomed as no living being had ever seen it. Trees put on several years' growth in a couple of months. Flowers made French landscapes of western horizons.

The first effects of global warming had become apparent to laypeople, if not to scientists. A chunk of Antarctica the size of Rhode Island broke off from the ice shelf, but authorities said it wasn't really a global warming effect, and everyone forgot about it. The hottest year on record? Well, maybe that indicated something. The hurricanes and tornadoes and floods were as mighty as any. Rainstorms swamped entire counties. Something was happening, and privately it worried people.

There was economic meltdown in Russia and Asia. Thailand, Indonesia, the Philippines, and Korea had all started to slide. That infernal factor of "saving face" wouldn't let Tokyo admit it, but Japan's economy hit bottom.

Jim started to get e-mails from pals at IBM and the big banks, as well as from info systems managers he had met at conferences. Every-where, the story was the same: "Batten down, twister coming. This will be the Real Big One." The drumbeat was less and less muffled—for those who listened.

Everyone was working long hours, but there was no way chaos could be avoided. It was time to start thinking about emergency preparedness, to do some contingency planning. Jim ordered a water storage tank and two big containers for fuel, and he invested in freeze-dried food—enough to keep Kate and him OK for a month, come what may. He promised himself he would have standbys for everything that ran on electricity, and some left over to help others.

Soon he started holding small meetings throughout the Valley, usually just in a friend's house, with some neighbors invited to drop by. At these gatherings, Jim sized up the Y2K picture as best he could, and advised people to lay in ten days' worth of necessary supplies—food, water, batteries, candles—and to remain rational. Some accepted his advice with good cheer. Others, perhaps a majority, thought he'd gone around the bend.

In early February, the White House called again. "Mr. Martin, I'd like to extend an invitation to you on behalf of the president, to come to Washington to join the President's Council on Year 2000 Conversion as a senior staff member. The offer is effective immediately. We recognize your financial independence, and we wouldn't, uh, insult you by offering you a salary as a consultant. We'd like to make you a dollar-a-year man—you might know that in the Roosevelt era, captains of industry consulted government by that arrangement. We will express mail you a letter of confirmation and a few necessary forms to fill out. Please take your time, but we would appreciate your reply within a week."

Jim listened carefully. He had expected something almost like this, but following the hints Woody had dropped, he was more than slightly suspicious of the White House's true motivations, and equally suspicious that the job offered would be more PR show than substantive action.

He opted for diplomacy. "I really appreciate your offer, sir. And I'll think about it seriously. But to tell you the truth, I believe I can be more useful to the president and the council out here at the grass roots than sitting at a desk in Washington. That's never been my style, but I'm honored by your consideration."

The next morning a round-robin letter from a Denver woman caught his attention as he scrolled through his e-mails:

> *I am convinced we are looking at the lights of a head-on freight train straight in the face. I am doing everything I can to get people to see the light here. I have noticed a lot of people are in denial about this, and they can almost be obstinate . . . What will anything else matter if this thing goes in the direction it appears to be heading?!*
>
> *You would be surprised at the different sorts of people who are arming themselves, and the fear they have. I believe the good Lord gave us a sound mind, and whatever comes of this, we are to use it.*

Please stay in touch with me . . . it is a comfort to know others during these times.

God Bless, Joanna

Jim e-mailed her back some words of encouragement. Good people, he mused. Maybe a bit too doomsdayish for my taste, but to each their own.

As winter slipped into spring, and then summer, Jim was now sure the answer to Y2K lay simply in preparedness . . . *simply*. It would never be simple to overcome public apathy, complacency, even the surge of prosperity the stock market had unleashed. The American attention span was shortening every day. Oh, maybe 20 percent of the population would stockpile, no more. And they wouldn't do so till the crunch came. Finally, no one was yet talking publicly about the long-term "knock-on effect" of the Millennium Bug. Jim shuddered.

It was increasingly clear to him Y2K wouldn't wait until January 1 to show up. Nor would it go away on January 3, or even on December 3, 2000. It was a long-term problem to be lived with for years, which would be possible as long as people were prepared and resolute, and not apt to take up arms to defend their little patch.

As he reflected on the Denver e-mail, he realized more surely than before that he belonged out here with the people. Where he felt most comfortable was in the smaller cities and towns, the rural areas that Washington and the power players tended to patronize.

The following day, with no hesitation, Jim formally declined the offer to work with the President's Council. With his refusal, he sent his deep thanks.

As 1998 began slipping by, the nation became preoccupied with the baseball season, the sleaze in Washington, and euphoria over the surging stock market. It seemed to Jim that little was being done, at least in public view, about Y2K.

Behind the scenes, people of good intent acknowledged the problem; those in a position to do so were scrambling to fix what they could. But they knew that the fix might create even more complex problems, especially if they had no time to test out the systems, and that thorough testing required a full year.

Those in the executive branches of government—federal, state, and local—were doing what they did best: saying, with forced confidence, they would "handle everything." But too often they seemed to be stonewalling. They admitted nothing. They were "ready," even if some of their systems were not compliant. Over the previous year, the number of "mission critical" systems the federal government absolutely had to fix to permit its continued operation dropped, without explanation, from more than 8,000 to 4,000, after which progress reports looked indeed promising. Clearly, the Washington spinmeisters were "creating" progress by playing with numbers.

Worse, non–mission-critical systems were nowhere addressed. The implication—that businesses could operate smoothly without remediating these systems—simply whistled citizens past the graveyard. A race car in which six of the ten spark plugs are dysfunctional would never even get out onto the track. And truth be known, non–mission-critical systems make up about 60 percent of all business systems.

Far too many authorities had not taken Y2K seriously enough to avoid disruptions. As 1999 loomed, Washington made an admission of sorts when it shifted its spin from Y2K *awareness* to Y2K *preparedness.* Increasingly, government agencies such as the Federal Emergency Management Agency (FEMA) and now the American Red Cross, advised people to prepare on their own and to avoid relying on officialdom. The message was the same to local governments: Coordinate your actions and don't count on Washington. The latter portion of the message turned even more poignant when it became known that the District of Columbia was so far behind in preparedness that it might simply grind to a halt in the new millennium—unless Congress authorized speedy, major outlays. And if DC came to a halt, chances were that federal government would do the same.

Business and industry? Sure, the private sector looked pretty good—with the emphasis on pretty—but there was not enough time to check the remediation that had been done. And how domestic commerce fared depended on other factors, like supplier-vendors and foreign partners, who may or may not have ignored the problem.

In late autumn, Jim heard that some major industrial giants were simply abrogating the task of bringing their systems into compliance. One large oil company was at least honest enough to admit it would not be able to fix 100 percent of its systems in time; the costs of remediation were enormous. Other businesses decided, without fanfare, on the calculated-risk policy "Fix on Failure," which meant exactly what it said. In so doing, they guaranteed the probability of breakdowns.

Jim was also suspicious of the Y2K business practice called "due diligence." It was buck-passing on a grand scale: a manufacturer, for example, required a letter from all its suppliers promising they had done everything in their power to avoid Y2K disruptions, and that they were compliant to help them bottomline. True, some of the majors had actually gone out to inspect vendors, certifying those that would be OK, canceling contracts with those who lagged. The policy had even acquired a name—"fortressing." Medium-size businesses, however, simply had to rely on the due diligence letter.

Those in the private economic sector who would be hit hardest, everyone agreed, were small-business people—employers of half the workforce in America—for they were at the mercy of all the systems that could go wrong, and had no way to prepare outside of their own areas of operation. A function as simple as accounts receivable could go down the tubes for relatively small outfits if links in the financial chain went askew, which could mean curtains for artisans, builders, shopkeepers, local restaurants, garages, even the few mom-and-pop stores that survived.

In all this mix of the intertwined economy, no one really knew what the total cost of fixing the Y2K Bug worldwide would be. But it was well up in the hundreds of billions of dollars—probably over one trillion. And then there was the additional $1 to $2 trillion that sources estimated would be the total of legal liability suits filed as a result of Y2K. Canny trial lawyers attended business conferences, hired PR flacks and promoters, and publicized their street smarts. They signed up clients by the planeload, and guaranteed themselves better incomes than they had had ambulance-chasing, while Congress wrestled with bills to insulate businesses from an avalanche of torts.

Jim's train of thought continued. All these calculations ignored the likelihood that Y2K was going to alter life well into the next century. We had not yet grasped its full meaning, if indeed we dared to contemplate the awesome facts. Soon we would have to face the realities. That was why it was so necessary to get the message out that there was nothing to fear, that Y2K was a clarion call to us all.

CHAPTER SIX

Manzanita Ranch
January 1999

One of the many booming Y2K Internet sites carried a 1998 year-end wrap-up—a nonscientific guesstimate of preparedness as the clock clicked over to 365 days. Jim scrolled through the personal accounts in the summary, his face grim. Two, in particular, caught his eye. The first:

> *I spoke with my bank (US Bank in Portland) and asked them about buying gold and silver coins. The bank employee looked at me and asked, "Y2K?" and I responded, "Yes." She told me I was about the 150th person this month to inquire about the conversion of assets to gold. She advised me to call the brokerage division of the bank.*

The second account was equally interesting:

> *At Grand Union in Smithtown, New York, I had a clerk recently ask me if we were invaded or something, because so many*

> *people had packed the store for the canned goods sale. At Waldbaums in Ronkonkoma, when they put 20-lb. bags of rice on sale (about once a month), they fly out the door. I saw one lady buying three.*

Jim sat back, massaged his temples. It was clear folks weren't getting the necessary messages, and that some people—media—weren't getting these messages out because certain other people—government—weren't seeing to it that they did.

The rice bags flying out the door bothered him the most. People just *had* to understand how it worked, had to be *told* how it worked—that the average supermarket stocked enough food to meet normal demand for three days in case deliveries were delayed. If shoppers suddenly bought large quantities, the shelves would be stripped the first day and empty the next two, rather than creating panic. If shoppers stocked up gradually, rather than all together at the last minute, the flow of goods would remain constant.

This craziness happened every year on the East Coast, Jim reflected, any time a hurricane approached; unable to stockpile larger-than-normal quantities of water or batteries or plywood, stores were instantly stripped bare, and the rush spread in concentric circles. Evidently, a discouraging number of people never got the message from the "big gasoline shortage" in the early seventies, when the same thing happened. The rate of supply was normal, but motorists *thought* there was, or would be, a shortage, and they rushed the pumps, changing their buying patterns from filling up at a quarter tank to filling up, and topping off, at a three-quarter tank. They *created* the "shortage"—long lines, short tempers, congestion, fear . . . sometimes panic.

Now he could see everything falling into place and leading to the same pointless, and dangerous, scenario. Another little piece of history that, if forgotten, we were surely doomed to repeat.

Once again en route to Washington, Jim stopped off in Champaign, Illinois, to compare notes with geeks who had struck the mother lode by starting up a remediation consulting company at just the right time. Ken Moore, an old buddy from IEMS days, invited Jim home for dinner. They drove south out of the scruffy center of the Midwestern university town, through February snow, along an avenue of houses with rocking-chair porches and trees that would soon be large with leaf. Then they broke out past a huge cheese-processing plant, to the mall-and-condo jigsaw that stretched across the flat prairie. Jim peered at a shopping center like every other in Anywhere USA, curious to see what Middle America was up to. Ken mistook the glance. "I know. Unless I sit and think, I sometimes can't even remember where I live. It all looks so much the same."

Jim tensed. "There's a crowd over there. Let's take a look."

Ken parked the car and they got out. Jim shouldered up to a man in sheepskin coat and overalls, with a Caterpillar cap on his head, flaps down.

"They get something new in?" Jim asked.

"Generators. Said they'd sell to the first fifty customers, then close the doors. That's it. No more this millennium." He actually cackled. "Me, I got here at three-thirty. Gettin' up early ain't no problem. Got mine, all right! Figured I'd stick around, see what happens." He seemed embarrassed at having to own up to his desire to linger and gawk. Then he added, "Aw shucks. Might be better than on TV, y'know? They had a line, nice and orderlylike, then. Just now it looked to turn nasty. Cops should be here yet."

Jim glanced over at a well-dressed woman—an artful, million-dollar real estate agent, or maybe an academic—trying to press forward but repulsed by the increasingly agitated crowd. He sauntered over.

"I heard they have a shipment of water storage tanks in," she remarked. "Oh, I just hope . . ."

Jim told her this crowd was about generators. Her face fell. "Oh, I can't cope with things like that! Maybe some nice man could help me?"

Just as Jim felt he was about to be recruited, Ken came up, apologized for the intrusion, and drew him aside, pointing to a man in three-button charcoal gray. "I asked him what he was here for. Said he didn't know what they were selling but that anytime he notices a line, he figures it's worth looking into, just to see what he might come up with."

"A guy like that, into this kind of scene?" Jim shook his head. "It's like those Internet auctions. Or maybe more like Russia, where folks join a line automatically, figuring whatever's available is valuable. Sometimes they leave with a loaf of bread, or an orange."

Ken grinned as they headed for the car. "We aren't that bad off . . . yet."

"I'm not so sure. Let me read you an e-mail I got just before I left:

> *A few weeks ago, diesel generators were readily available in the southern AZ area. Now there are none to be found. We are looking for one (obviously we waited too long), and my husband remembered a large lumber/building supply store in a small town that always has a good supply of all kinds of generators (they service contractors). He drove up there today and found they had one generator, a small five-hundred-watt gas type, on the shelf.*

After Champaign, Jim flew on to Washington. Having turned down the White House, he'd made it his business to get close to the Senate subcommittee on Y2K matters, and to its chairman, Senator Ezra Palmer, who had responded by inviting Jim to testify at a hearing on the Hill.

The subcommittee's press secretary, Susan, told Jim she had billed him as "one of the good ole boys—a guy who was onto Y2K from the start." Then she gloomily played a tape of reactions that took place when she alerted the networks to the problem:

> *Get real! You're talking stuff that might happen almost a year from now. It's already overhyped anyway. Big scare. So what?*

> *Sure, the country goes down the tubes every day, regularly, at five o'clock. That doesn't justify me sending another crew down to the Hill.*

Thanks. We can take it off C-SPAN.

Forget it. The American public still believes in the great American technological fix. If we can put a Rover on Mars, we can fix a few computer bugs down here on planet Earth. Right? When you have something solid, get back with me!

Even CNN declined. Susan finally got some iffy interest from National Public Radio, and thought she might get a couple of sound bytes on commercial radio. Maybe even a clip or two on the overnight TV news shows. But that was all.

After the hearing in the near-empty chamber that afternoon, Senator Palmer ushered Jim into a comfortably old-fashioned inner sanctum. Jim loved the smell of the leather polish; instinctively, he looked around for a spittoon.

"How do you think it went?" Palmer asked.

"OK, I guess. But I sure would've liked to see some big media, and maybe more witnesses."

"Susan did her best. For the newsies, it's either a ho-hum or launch the torpedoes. They live by handout and they follow the pack. Too damn little initiative in the mix." Then Palmer brightened a bit. "We need to get the word out beyond the National Press Club and the Beltway. We need a hundred guys like you going around the country talking turkey out at the grass roots. That's where the crunch will come—out there." Palmer made a sweeping gesture. "Too many folks still in denial."

A couple of other senators trickled in, followed shortly by three senior members of the House. A woman and young man, both of whom Jim remembered from the President's Council on Year 2000 Conversion, slipped in almost surreptitiously. The young man fixed Jim in his inscrutable gaze; she smiled thinly. Jim nodded at both.

Senator Palmer asked them, "You pretty sure no one saw you?"

The White House woman glanced at Jim and replied, "We're pretty good at diversion down there these days, Mister Chairman."

Senator Palmer called for order. "OK, ladies and gentlemen. I believe you all know Jim Martin. He has come to give us some in-country examples of what's happening out there."

Jim looked at the chairman and plunged in. "What I'm getting as I travel is . . . I guess you'd call it querulousness. People have too many questions, not enough answers. Too much fear, verging on panic, like I saw yesterday in Illinois." Jim told the story of the mall store and the crowd. His audience listened politely.

"Here's another. I checked back with a woman in the Denver area I first heard from a while ago. Since she started trying to organize her neighborhood, she said her phone has been ringing off the hook. The comments she's been receiving are as follows." He removed a piece of paper from his shirt pocket, unfolded it, and read:

> *"To answer your question—yes, it is going better than I would have ever expected, but not because of the government, and forget the state.*
>
> *"Our program is going strong.*
>
> *"It's very interesting to me how each person has begun to prepare.*
>
> *"I am an RN and I keep telling others at work about Y2K. At first, they kidded me like all get-out! Now they are working on their own plans. I have learned a great deal about human nature during this time. I don't personally believe this will be only a bump on the road. Believe we'll see more than our grandparents ever saw.*
>
> *"My husband and I have a little farm out on the prairie, with a well on it. We plan to go there because I have a mother who must have oxygen. The only way we can keep it working if the electricity goes down is with a generator. That will take a lot of fuel, which we would be unable to store in the city. Of course, I've opened the farm to others, and they're coming, all right, and helping us get ready.*

> "I knew some would plan to leave and some would plan to stay. Many are going home to parents. Those who stay have offered to watch over the homes. I know there will be others who will need a home and food, and I will be as ready as possible to help them. Before I met all these people, I wouldn't have known what to do exactly. Now I can see that only together will we be able to survive this.
>
> "We don't know how severe it will be, but one thing we do know is, we will be in God's service during those uncertain times!"

"She's making preparations," Senator Palmer commented, "and she's caring for her neighbors. That's the message I think we want to get out."

Jim glanced at Palmer, then said, "Maybe twenty percent of Americans realize Y2K may affect their lives. But I'd guess that less than ten percent are making preparations. Now that the media hype has died down, people aren't getting a clear message from Washington that they need to get ready—and that the federal government isn't going to help them out of this one.

"I still believe an informed public is America's best defense. With all due respect, I'd ask you to get some sense of urgency into your information releases. Also, the more we know, the more it appears that Y2K will be lasting a long time. I gotta admit I'm seriously worried about the short- to medium-term social and economic effects."

Senator Palmer, who had been on the Hill for a considerable while, caught the tension among the small group of listeners. "It's the domino effect we really have to concern ourselves with," he explained. "We're operating in a vacuum."

A congresswoman spoke up. "But this Y2K thing is immediate. We have a date certain. And then you layer on top of it all the madness associated with century change—not to mention the millennium, which alone is going to lead to irrational behavior. There'll be a hell of a lot of wild parties around the country, too. And the FBI has warned of terrorist acts at New Year's."

The woman from the White House interjected, "There's another disturbing aspect to this. You've probably all heard reports that Y2K computer programmers are quitting and heading for the hills. Or they want to be paid in cash only—and it's not to evade taxes. These people are talking Armageddon."

"Yeah," Jim cut in, "we have Steinharts out where I am. He was a high-powered professor of computer sciences at Stanford. Maybe you saw them on TV—survivalists. They're building a self-contained type of fortress up in the mountains. And I've heard he's got weapons, ready to fight off anyone who might come looking to get at his stockpile—"

The White House woman continued as if she hadn't heard Jim. "They circulate bulletins purporting to be Department of Defense (DOD) documents, that indicate the Marines, Army, and National Guard are running mobilization exercises to contain large-scale civil disorder. Their story is, they're expecting a repeat of Los Angeles nineteen ninety-two, only on a national scale."

"Another thing," Jim offered. "You all know that a lot of the top government programmers are going over to private industry. These guys stuck with government, hoping they could do some good; but now they're so disgusted, they're giving up pension rights to go for the money those Y2K consultant firms offer—like several hundred dollars an hour. That's leaving some federal and state agencies in a hell of a bind . . . right now, at crunch time."

To Palmer's right, Senator Dugger, a White House loyalist Democrat and the minority vice-chairman of the Y2K subcommittee, sat nodding. When not diverted by the impeachment trial, the pair of senior senators had been devoting their time to Y2K for more than a year now, and were as one on everything concerning the approaching crisis.

"You can bet the TV shows will pick all this up soon," Dugger said, "and play it hard. Y2K panic—big talking point on the squishy talk shows. They'll push that button real hard, again and again. It's the same-old same old: the major networks and newspapers, and the weekly news magazines, let the tabs lead. Then they plead they can't ignore a story that grabs the guts of an entire nation. They go into reckless and inflammatory coverage, and the consequences be damned. All that matters to them are ratings points and market share."

Palmer took the lead again. "Our answer has to be to try to bring good, solid American common sense out of the closet. And get people into a posture of rational preparedness."

There was a blank stillness in the room—the kind that happens when no one has answers. The chairman looked around. "When you have something visibly terrible, like a tornado or a flood or a hurricane, people pull together. With this situation, nothing seems to arouse the public. The first wave of interest, at the start of the year as the media blitzed it, has fizzled. People's attention has gone elsewhere. Y2K is too remote. The only thing we know is, it's going to start happening on that certain date."

The blanket of quiet in the room grew heavy. Jim looked a question at Senator Palmer. "With the chairman's permission," he said, "I'd like to come back to an uncomfortable point I touched on earlier. We have to be very clear that we're dealing not with just a few events that will happen on or about January first, two thousand. No way. What Y2K really means is a series of disruptions of differing severity, like a tornado touching down in unforeseen places at unpredictable times, and continuing for an indeterminate period. Power disruptions and economic slowdown may not appear until spring or summer."

Senator Palmer shot a look of inquiry at Jim, then nodded permission for him to continue. "The tornado analogy isn't a bad one insofar as frequency is concerned, although Y2K events won't be that vicious. They'll upset the pattern of life as we know it. And they'll continue, most likely, for weeks, possibly months. This is the *true* domino effect."

Jim noticed that whereas some of those present seemed absorbed in the scenario he was presenting, others were getting impatient. Was he telling them things they didn't want to hear? He continued, undaunted. "Raw materials will start to come in hiccups, including imports of manufactured goods. Our export trade may slump more than it already has. Our trade deficit will probably go through the roof at the end of ninety-nine and early into two thousand. Remember, some countries haven't even started to remediate; others scoff at the thought. When the squeeze comes, Developing World populations that are already hostile because they believe we deprive them on purpose . . ." He paused, then added, nodding to the White House people, "Well, that's more your bailiwick than mine—but I reckon if they get angry enough, some of them may be capable of pretty serious action against us.

"Still I have great faith—and a number of other people working on the problem do, too—that our brainpower and our resolve will overcome the challenges as they occur. We'll think up new solutions to new problems. I guess the physicists will have a field day because we'll be living out their theories of chaos and complexity . . . I think of the Great Depression, which my dad used to describe to me. There was misery, sure. And it hit almost everyone here; then it hit the rest of the world. This one might work the other way around—hitting the rest of the world first, then coming home to roost.

"Our success in meeting this challenge will hinge partly on our determination not to crumble in fear of what is happening around us. And this we can do by recognizing that Y2K might change many aspects of our lives *for the better!* If we have the sense to seize the opportunity. What can block our efforts is panic, not only here at home but worldwide.

"Maybe it's naive of me to think this, but I suspect we'll go through a period of chaos, perhaps hardship, and emerge into an era of untold prosperity. How long it will last—well, that's anyone's guess."

He was finished, but there were no further questions or comments, nothing. He waited another few seconds, then said, "Thanks for listening."

Jim flew back into Santa Barbara, where he retrieved his car. He drove up the winding road over San Marcos Pass so deep in thought he almost strayed into the path of a tourist bus thundering downhill. As he crested the pass, he basked in the sight of the stark mountains cascading down to form the neck of the Santa Ynez Valley. Ahead lay man-made Lake Cachuma, the main source of water for many communities in the county—as long as the pumps worked. He wondered whether this pristine fastness would be spared invasion by marauding hoards of city people in search of food and shelter in the times to come.

The Halloweenish California oaks, bowed and knotted, were now endangered by vineyard owners who wanted to clear ever more land for their grapes. The knobby, smoothly ground moraines, whose slopes captured just the right angles of sun to add flavor to the grapes of summer, stood gaunt and brooding. Once-golden aspens had been shorn of all but a few maroon leaves.

Jim thought of the Chumash casino, which provided welcome income for the sprawling coastal-and-inland tribe. The Mission Indians could now drive shiny pickups and SUVs to attend services at Mission Santa Ines. Here, too, there were farmers who specialized in growing natural foods, ranchettes with corrals for riding horses, and toney private schools. In the village of Santa Ynez there were shops as yet too small to have been invaded by mall-mongers, and Danish descendants over in Solvang who lassoed tourists by the busload with sticky baked goods and neo-Frisian facades.

Thinking of these people—from the comfortably well-off to the leathery Indian-Hispanic cowboys—Jim was momentarily daunted by the task of trying to bring them together to face Y2K. But, he mused, the problem here is no different from the task facing those in larger towns and cities who sought to organize response and to defeat fear.

The trip to Washington had been a downer. Meeting skepticism on the Hill was a real disappointment. He had expected there, of all places, he would be dealing with cold reality, not impatience because the day's concerns were more pressing.

When Jim got back to the little ranch, he greeted Kate with as much warmth as he could muster, ate a quick supper, and did something he had not done since boyhood: he climbed into bed and pulled the covers over his head. So much to do. So little time. And so hampered by complacency.

One of the vice president's planning staff, alert to Y2K's possible effect on Campaign 2000, stumbled on Jim's name while scrolling through reports from the White House Council. There his eye stopped roving. As soon as he could, he grabbed his boss's attention.

"Here's this guy, Mister Vice President, who knew all about Y2K twenty years ago. He isn't in politics, but he sure might be able to do some pretty effective advance damage control for us. I'd suggest, sir, that you call him to see if maybe he'll come back to Washington for an informal meeting."

"Maybe," replied the veep. "Check out what they think of him over at the Council. Also see if he's clean."

"Already done, sir. He's a registered Republican, known to be straight-arrow. I checked around on the Hill. He's been working with the Senate Y2K subcommittee in an informal capacity for a while. Gets on very well with Senator Palmer, the Majority chair, and Senator Dugger. Good reputation on both sides of the aisle.

"Although he's not particularly interested in politics, he's very concerned about national security in the broadest sense. He's friends with the Democratic state assemblywoman for his district, and her husband. So, Martin gets pretty high marks all around. Another thing, he turned down an official offer from the Year 2000 Council folks. 'Don't want to get involved in the bureaucracy,' he said."

"Sounds like an interesting guy. OK, set it up."

The staffer phoned Jim to alert him that he would receive a call the following morning from the vice president. Jim quickly phoned Woody.

Woody's take was succinct and complete: the vice president of course had an office at the Senate, which he rarely used. His real, official staff worked in the Executive Office Building on technology matters, presidential backup, foreign visits, and the like. The second staff, less public yet still announced and in operation, handled his campaign for the presidency in year 2000 out in the open, but not on official premises. Then there was a third group of staffers—forming a sort of think tank—who worked out of a discreet office building in far northwest Washington. In many ways, this was the most important of the three, because it housed the group of hardheads who game-planned policies to move the veep to the year 2000 Democratic presidential nomination, and thence into the White House.

Woody had heard the publicity-shy campaign staff was seriously worried that, next to Yugoslavia and Iraq and wildcat terrorism, Y2K might have a disastrous effect on their man's campaign. "My bet is, they're the fellows who called you. They stay out of sight, but they're the brains behind the campaign. Tough to deal with. Slippery customers. Slash and burn. I'd watch my step if I were in your shoes.

"Polls can't tell them anything worthwhile, because this is such a vague issue. And without polling these days, a Washington pol doesn't know his ass from deep center field, does he?" Jim thought he heard Woody chuckle softly at the other end of the phone line.

"I mean," Woody went on, "what if Y2K blew big just around California primary time—say, in March two thousand? And then conditions continued to get worse, right through into September, getting close to the election? That's what you call a *real* wild card. No wonder those fellers are a little nervous.

"And how would they feel about you if you hadn't fed them absolutely straight, incontrovertible info? Don't you think heads would roll—yours among them? Hell, it would be a bloodbath! Stay out of it, my friend, is the best advice I can give you. Stay clean."

So, Jim thought when the conversation was over, the what-if scenarios were, politically speaking, nuclear. The vice president could invoke no fortressing strategy to avoid the fallout from Y2K. If it erupted into a major series of events next year, the Millennium Bug could destroy his long-cherished ambition.

Even more ironic, Jim mused, was the fact that the veep was a techie at heart. Now the risk was that he might be brought down by technological happenstance—a wild card indeed.

Brighton Beach, New York
Spring 1999
Over the previous decade or so, the Brooklyn enclave of Brighton Beach had become more Russian than Moscow. Back on the steppes, there was progress toward a new society of retro communists, forward-thinking bankers, and crooks. At times there was confusion over the dividing line between the last two categories. In Brooklyn on the Bay, there were only high- and low-type gangsters, no political ideology.

The Brighton Beach ghetto had become headquarters of the Russian Mafia—the Org—a juicy, near-impenetrable target for the FBI and a multitude of other agencies that worry about crime, smuggling, subversion, and related nefarious deeds. What most grabbed and resonated with the Bureau was that the men from Moscow and environs were more greedy and ruthless than the Italians, Israelis, Colombians, Chinese, or Southeast Asians had ever dreamed of being. But then, the Ruskies had lost a lot of time under Krushchev and Brezhnev and Andropov, when travel was not free and the KGB kept a militantly beady eye on lowlife. When the Bureau politely asked the CIA to check with its contacts in the Mob to discover if any hanky-panky was underway between Russians and new-generation mafiosi, the Agency replied, just as courteously, that it was forbidden by law to provide information on domestic events.

Now, on balmy evenings, behind steamed windows arched with enameled Cyrillic lettering, the coffee rooms and old-guard restaurants of Brighton Beach stuttered with harsh gutturals and machine-gun–like consonants. Customers in shapeless, knee-length overcoats, fedoras—even astrakhans—sat with cups of tea, smoking the long-barreled *mahorka,* although Marlboros were plentiful and tax-free cheap. Occasionally, they burrowed deeper inside themselves to cough gutturally into cell phones, discussing this or that ploy with the high-flying Moscow nephews they had set up in the banking business after Boris had been propped up on a tank long enough to announce he was taking over.

In the corner of one such *shabeen,* a white-haired, full-bearded émigré strummed his balalaika and sang mournfully of the Moscow metro murals, of kolkhozes and apparatchiks. The patrons were the oldsters, redolent of soggy cabbage, black rye bread, garlic-blood sausage, and the smoke of the steppes. Among them were the senior brains of the new global octopus—sometimes also referred to as Papus. Some skulls belonged to former generals, lieutenant generals, and colonel generals of the former KGB of the former Soviet Union, who had opted to augment their outstanding pensions. They were, at the moment, in Brooklyn—not in Miami, for which they had developed a warped affection weirdly reminiscent of their puzzling love for Sochi on the Black Sea, except for the times business called them to Florida to deal with Cuban stepchildren, who didn't know how to make tea or bread.

Since the Russian state suffered from a chronic inability to compensate anyone who tried to be honest, the former high officers made common cause with colleagues still in the ranks, who more than happily opened the archives and the operating files to their Brooklyn-based brethren. Indeed, the alliance extended to other matters of operational utility, such as tools of the trade, transportation, false documents—in short, the trivia needed to operate sub rosa in formerly enemy territories.

In a gaudy nightclub across the street, the Org's slicked-down, buffed-up younger generation made the scene—postpubescent Dimitris and Alexeis and Sashas, untainted by daylight, which never encroached on their twisted lives, strutting their loosely leashed perversions for all to behold. The other pimply youths nodded sagely and continued to pick their teeth with Sheffield steel stilettos, a newly "in" item. They rapped in a mixture of street Russian, skinhead German, ghetto English. And they often came close to public rape, indifferent to the sex of their target.

In the nightclub's corners, the twenty-five–to–thirtyish, slightly superior, blasé new capos watched their soldiers crow like banty roosters. As they sluiced down vodka flavored with habaneros or thyme or poppy seed, they plotted to overthrow their elders.

The oldsters' East Coast corridor gas-station scam had bilked Washington out of millions in taxes by the simple tactic of buying discount brand stations, selling quantities of gas, neglecting to pay taxes, and selling the stations before the authorities could close in. A measure of the gas station swag found its way into the ever-holed Gen-X pockets. Their careless wealth, in turn, attracted juicy babushkas from the porn circuit in Moscow—even occasional American-grown chicks who, it turned out, never could absorb the patois of Brighton's streets.

After some delicate intergenderal negotiations, the nimble brains of both the Papus and the youngsters were now joined in concentration on meatier targets. Russians, at home wherever they were, read the papers and watched the news. The Org was well aware that Host America was skittish as it prepared fitfully for a shortage economy they called Y2K.

The wise, kindly looking old men had ordered most of the huge profits of their gasoline scam relaundered into large and small banks across the country. Russians with management smarts then moved into action.

Their plan was simple: it centered on two houses that had been gutted and unostentatiously remodeled so that their shabby exteriors belied the intense, high-tech offices they contained. One headquarters was in Brighton Beach, the other in Wichita, Kansas, to which had been dispatched those Orgniks most able to pass as Americans or Germans. From both, a stream of communications had moved the operation into high gear by the start of 1999. The plan, quite simply, was to corner the American market in survival gear.

To help shortages materialize, Org soldiers indulged in judicious schemes. Occasionally, trucks swerved into inexplicable accidents. Container loads of camp stoves and kerosene lamps were flooded with corrosives. Two fully-stocked warehouses burned mysteriously. Several companies that manufactured freeze-dried foods for adventurers and wilderness trekkers found their raw materials cut off, and others suffered serious damage to production facilities. Motors were seized up; sugar appeared where it was not needed. Conflicting purchase orders streamed into vendors' offices. Bills of lading were missing. Overdue payments never made it to the designated banks. Quite simply, the routines of shortage-supply commerce were screwed up.

Yet some orders were genuine, and were paid for impeccably. The supplies went into anonymous, well-wired and guarded warehouses near truck terminals in places like Memphis, Indianapolis, and Los Angeles.

Much of the intricate work was performed by computer geeks drafted by the Org from the missile programs of the former Red Army and from the ex-Soviet equivalent of the National Security Agency. The Russian Mafia also had the most useful forgers, safecrackers, thieves, con men, and cardsharpers sprung from jails, taught a language other than catarrh, polished for export, and put to work where they were needed—or simply held in reserve.

It didn't take long for the Org to make a dent in the survival business.

CHAPTER SEVEN

Manzanita Ranch
March 1999

Late one night, Jim returned home from a Central California speaking gig on rural preparedness for Y2K. A state senator had gathered reps from ten counties and from over a hundred rural communities up and down the length of the state, and Jim's message hit home. No one had previously bothered to talk to villages so small they barely counted on the political map.

Next morning, the vice president's border-state tones mellowed down the satellite link from the office on Connecticut Avenue. "OK, Jim. Let's cut to the chase. How do you see Y2K? Could this thing really blow up in our faces before the election?"

Jim breathed in, and launched. "The key question, sir, is: *Does Washington know what's going on?* Are you people inside the Beltway out of touch with the mood of the people? Are you interpreting your opinion polls correctly? This thing is subtle. It hasn't yet fully hit the consciousness of all the folks. Second, you people in Washington must understand how serious the Y2K situation could be. But there's no public evidence that the feds are doing serious preparation except, if you'll pardon the expression, to cover their asses. The bureaucrats just—"

The vice president zapped right through Jim's head of steam. "What do we *do*? I know we have some political differences, but I'm still asking for your help. What I'm saying is, we need a real, gilt-edge assessment and firm policy recommendations from someone out there among the plain folks."

"Who's *we*, Mr. Vice President? You as an officer of government or you as a candidate?"

The veep rode straight over that one too, continuing the recruitment pitch. "Can you do it in a month—two months max? Tell Frank what you need and we'll get it for you."

Jim bridled at the VP's presumption. "Mr. Vice President, I want you to understand two things. One, I probably won't vote for you, although for the good of the country I might be prepared to do what you ask. And two, I'm not in this for money. I want you to understand that."

"OK, good man! I'll be counting on you, Jim. Thanks. Talk to you again soon, I hope." *Click.*

Over the next few days, two letters arrived in Jim's mailbox, each in a plain envelope, each stamped rather than franked by machine. They were both addressed To Whom It May Concern, directing them to assist James Martin of Los Olivos, California, in his inquiries on behalf of the undersigned into the possible effects of Y2K. One was on official vice presidential stationery; the other, under the letterhead of the candidate's campaign office.

Kate whooped with excitement, then subsided when Jim told her she couldn't make a big deal out of it with her friends. How he wished Beth were there to see the letters and the signatures. *Maybe she can after all,* he concluded.

In the seventy-two hours since his phone call from the VP, Jim had thought more about the mission he had agreed to. And he had become more dubious. Had the White House changed its stripes? Was topside now truly concerned about the effect of Y2K on the American people? Or had he been recruited as part of a purely political ploy? He felt uncomfortable now that he had the official documents in his hand. And he felt increasingly suspicious that the administration was intent on playing Y2K to its own advantage.

Over dinner that evening, Assemblywoman Danielle Johanssen, back from Sacramento for a weekend, listened and smiled. "So *that's* what it was all about! A couple of suits stormed my office this week, in a real hurry to find out everything we could tell them about you. We gave you pretty good grades. But I don't know if we did you a favor."

Early April 1999
Jim traveled, listened, and worked his report to the vice president. During the previous winter, the media storm of unease had grown from a mild breeze of apprehension to near-hurricane force; by spring, the storm had abated, although the atmosphere was still heavy. It amounted, as Senator Palmer had said back in Washington, to "terrorism of the mind." People began to react to the lack of solid information from credible sources. Their brains played insidious games.

Jim called Woody often, seeking guidance. They mulled over public perceptions, opinion management, even thought-control. Woody's anger boiled up whenever he talked of the media. "How sad, how shortsighted they are to underestimate the American public!" He discarded the usual plowshare lingo as he ripped into a real stem-winder. "The reprehensible media fringe! Guttersnipes! Working on tips and rumors! Treating gossip as news . . . Meanwhile, people out there are confused, complacent. They're hypnotized by the good times; they're on a consumer binge. They need a reality check. Need the truth, some knowledge of what might really happen.

"If they know the facts, they'll manage, never you fear! Our people got guts and resources the pols always underestimate. Only *someone's* got to be smart enough to tell them, straight. And I'm not sure this administration has the moxie to face those facts." Then he slumped verbally. "It's enough to make a feller want to resign from the world, ain't it?"

Washington, DC
Mid-April 1999

The first signs of public dismay prompted the President's Council on Year 2000 Technology Conversion to convene a high-level confabulation in the now familiar, still stodgy Old Executive Office Building, that ungainly relic of imperial America. Someone noted, as they trooped into a meeting room, that it was the fifty-fifth anniversary of FDR's death, but no one picked up on the remark to make an analogy. Jim attended as an observer, sponsored by the vice president's office. He nodded once again at his supercilious young interrogator and listened attentively.

"On the one hand," a member argued, "if we admit to what's really happening, we're going to feed panic."

"On the other hand," a political spin-control talent from the private sector responded, "you've already created a mess. Even fewer people trust government than did before, because you've left-footed this one all the way."

"So, what do we do?" asked a newly recruited civil servant. "There's pressure from topside to produce something. We're thinking of maybe a statement to back up the mention made in the State of the Union Address."

"Do we just come out and tell the people there's no way in hell either the public or private sector can be in total compliance?" asked another. "The basic question is, can the American people stand hearing the truth? If we let 'em have it, right between the eyes, are they going to panic? Buy up everything in sight, turn on each other? Or is there some way we can encourage them to use their common sense? To be prepared to take almost any disruption in stride? Mr. Martin, can you address that?"

"I can, sir," Jim replied. "Regardless of the spin, lots of communities have seen it coming and are doing a damn fine job of preparation. Montgomery County, Maryland—right here, outside the District—Lubbock, Texas. San Diego. Miami–Dade. A little place called Norfolk, Nebraska . . . It's probably too late for others to get fully organized in advance, but maybe we can give them at least a psychological boost."

"How about some money for federally assisted food stockpiling, maybe through FEMA?" someone suggested.

"FEMA is hamstrung by policies in their charter," Jim replied. "Their job is to respond to emergencies, not to prevent or prepare for them."

"DOD?" asked a senator.

"Do we really want to bring the Pentagon into planning for a purely civilian crisis?" Jim countered. It was more a statement than a question.

"And we have the trial lawyers," someone else griped. "They're already drooling over the liability settlements they'll get."

"So what do we do?" asked another, finally. "Warn the public it isn't going to be peaches and cream?"

"I vote we do nothing," said a Council staffer. "We write a statement for the boss, urging those who have not yet complied to get moving. We urge everyone to be prepared—perhaps not as subtly as before. Reinforce the message that it's up to them. Just short of telling them they're on their own. Which they are, dammit. OK?"

The Council staffer snapped his fingers and looked at the high-priced political consultant. "How about we organize town meetings across the country? Have community leaders and someone from the President's Council up there on stage, TV cameras rolling, telling everyone it's going to be OK. We'll be seen to have concern. People will be reassured. Problem disappears."

Jim looked with concealed disbelief at the naïveté of the young man. But to his surprise, most of the others nodded approval, glad someone had taken them off the hook.

The meeting adjourned. Jim strode across Lafayette Park to the

Hay-Adams—the hotel he'd chosen as his bunkhouse in Washington. He loosened his tie, kicked off his city shoes, and sunk into deep thought. Even the guys in the President's Council weren't getting it. Or if they were, this was Washington, where everything was politics as usual.

They interpreted their mission to be the organization of a cover-up. The Washington people were so cocooned in government-think, they didn't admit that the wave of popular cynicism about government, indeed about institutions generally, was already a barely restrained power. People nowadays were fully aware that national bodies didn't respond to their needs and hence were increasingly irrelevant. That disingenuousness deepened even more as folks realized the only solutions lay in their own communities—solutions to be fashioned by them, on their own.

Once disruptions really broke out, and people learned the Y2K dislocation could have been avoided back in the early 1970s—or corrected any time in the '80s and '90s—all hell might let loose. Or maybe the people at the meeting *did* know but wouldn't admit it publicly, even in a tightly held meeting. Jim guessed the White House was operating from pure political fear, trying to contain the genie it knew was struggling to come out of its bottle.

Sure, after first quarter 1999, when the initial wave of interest in Y2K had subsided, everyone had become euphoric because the market was consistently crashing through stratospheric barriers, unemployment was marginal, inflation barely a threat. Even Kosovo and Iran seemed to have cooled down, at least for now.

The ostrich syndrome was alive and well, Jim concluded. But a time of reckoning and blame-seeking inevitably had to come. And it could produce something unpredictable which, he assumed, the White House was well aware of. This must be why, in the time remaining, the administration and the Republicans were trying to present as many crowd-pleasers as they could. Were they really worried and just trying to play politics-as-usual? Jim stirred restlessly, unhappy at the turn his thoughts had taken.

There was something else Woody had passed along to him. Plans, he said, were well underway to build a federal Y2K control bunker near the White House, a command-and-control center to monitor and shape the government's response once Y2K struck. The feds had also, quietly yet emphatically, issued a "request"—something short of an order—to major trade associations to report compliance and any incidents to the center so that Washington would have an up-to-the-minute readout on the computer operations of the entire nation.

"And then," Woody had added, "they're proposing a computer-safety plan, which they say is going to be directed against cyberterrorism. Strikes me that once they've built such a big intercept apparatus, they will be able to monitor anything they want, anywhere on the Net. But who am I to know stuff like that?" Woody had sounded gruff, acerbic, yet also worried.

The command center was to be ready in October, and to shut down in June. "June, my foot," Woody had grumbled. "They're going to be there a lot longer than that, and they know it!"

In his hotel room, Jim pondered further. The need to get a forceful message out, urging calm preparation, increased daily. Bland government assurances brought pitfalls of their own: if people really believed the problem was solved, they could become even more complacent, and in good conscience. Where, Jim asked himself, is the balance between the two courses?

After his return home, he sat down and wrote these thoughts into his report for the vice president. Then he mailed it, registered. He heard no more from Washington. Not even an unofficial letter of thanks.

Washington, DC
Predawn, April 25, 1999
Chief systems engineer Harold Bracken yawned nervously, his body yearning for oxygen to ease the tension cramps. He swiveled in his cushy manager's chair and gazed at the banks of dials. He gnawed the inside of his cheek, then switched to his fingernails. He glanced at his watch, at the wall clock, and finally at the digital readout in front of him.

God, he asked himself, do I really *want* to know what will happen? His index finger hovered over a bright blue button somewhat larger than a quarter. Immediately next to it was its bright red mate.

The clocks headed on down: *00:02.34.1 . . . 02.33.57 . . . 56 . . .*

Harold prayed. Awkwardly. He was not used to invoking spiritual powers. He was an engineer; his faith was in science and technology. But recently he had begun to think the yin and yang of the ages might be linked in ways far beyond his comprehension.

No more time to reflect. *00:01.54.2 . . . 1 . . .* The scope of what he was about to do raced through his mind. He thought back to the gathering he had recently attended, of senior executives from the main electric utilities of the three national grid sectors—East, Middle, and West—plus representatives from Canada, plus suited and uniformed feds. It had been conducted with all the secrecy of an emergency National Security Council meeting, in the underground command post of the West Virginia mountains.

Harold recalled the speculation that there was no way in hell the electricity providers of North America could consistently meet normal demand after January 1, 2000, quite apart from the problem of reliable fuel supplies. The abject admission—in this debugged, tightly guarded headquarters cavern resurrected from the atomic age—was that inevitably some systems would go down, placing added demand on other sectors. Further, that increased demand on crippled facilities would lead to rolling brownouts, with metro Chicago an excellent case in point. The probability was that, unless the federal government moved into authoritarian mode, the electrical industry would have to buy extra power from brokers at prices higher than the 900-fold markup they had paid during recent major shortages—that is, if there *were* surplus power for sale anywhere. Finally, the reluctant consensus that the two nations would be lucky to get away with no more serious repercussions.

How long would it take to bring the grid back up to normal—and keep it there? The feds had pressured, insisting that all efforts be bent to remediation, even if there was no longer enough time to test.

The threat of emergency powers had hung, nearly palpable, over the tense meeting table.

"We don't know," the delegate from Austin had snorted, "because we can't test the sonofabitch in real time, can we? We're too scared of the panic it might cause. So what do we do?"

The consensus had been that everyone ought to renew an acquaintance with God, Buddha, Krishna, maybe a Mayan or Hopi spirit or two. There were thin cynical smiles around the table.

When he came back from the gathering, Harold Bracken pondered as long as his conscience would let him, finally deciding he owed it to the nation to test just how bad the breakdown would be. Which is why his fingers now hovered over the blue and red buttons. Blue would initiate the final trigger for the override program he had inserted in the Southwestern states control grid, a go-for-broke simulation of what would happen at Rollover—one second after midnight, January 1, 2000. Red overrode the override and kept the system humming normally.

Harold asked for final guidance from whatever power might exist in the beyond. He was drenched in rank sweat.

00:00.47.42 . . . 41 . . . 40 . . .

His hand wavered. He breathed deeply for the umpteenth time, rose from his chair, went to a blank wall next to a plate-glass window, and pulled down the handle that sealed the room from external terrorist attack.

00:00.28.49 . . . 48 . . . 47 . . .

How alone he was! Would he emerge charged with treason or celebrated as a Paul Revere? He knew it didn't matter. What mattered was the result of the test.

A flicker appeared in all the system readouts. Emergency power flipped on in the command post. Sirens and horns and warning bells went off. The backup generating system had clicked on; it was programmed to operate only locally, right here in the center. A sign, Harold had long thought, of the skepticism with which top executives regarded their systems' capabilities.

He glanced at the big electronic wall map of interconnections that made up the US and Canadian power grids. Shortages were rolling across the country! As power outed in the Southwest, other systems automatically adjusted to balance the entire network, east–west and north–south, diagonally. Blackened sectors and links popped up every which way as networks and generating stations strained to make up for the Southwest's shortfall in capacity. Some came on bright again pretty quickly. Others remained dark, even spread. Then a few of those that had come on, went off. The big board showed momentary chaos.

Harold sighed, pushed up the locking mechanism on the control-room door, and walked out, nearly bumping into the burly security guard.

"What's going on, Doc?" the guard asked.

"Major outage. I gotta talk to the boss. Stand by here. No one enters without amber clearance, got it?"

Harold hurried down the corridor, pulled out his cell phone, hit a memory button. He didn't pause for chitchat. "Don, we gotta talk. I'll meet you at that old drive-in, Hundred and Eighty-Seventh Street and Avenue F. About twenty minutes, OK? No screwing around. This is for real, as you may have realized. Be there!"

Las Vegas, Nevada
April 25, 1999
Night was stumbling toward dawn. On the harshly lit floors of Las Vegas casinos, no one noticed. The usual diehards, a few lushes, and the harpies who preyed on them all hung out at the tables. The big stage shows had long since folded. Families had gone upstairs to their tens of thousands of rooms in the plastic palaces that crowded out into the desert. Room service waitpeople yawned. Imported chefs read newspapers in their native languages. Showgirls slept wherever the cast of the die had landed them.

Lights flickered, then went out. Emergency power systems snapped in, keeping the hotels' vitals running: air-conditioning, two banks of prewired slot machines, wastewater. The lights on the gambling floor were off.

Assistant managers checked the hard copies of their emergency manuals and went into the prescribed drills. Then they waited, mystified. No sudden, desert thunderstorm—which sometimes knocked out power briefly—had passed through, at least not as far as they knew. Nor had there been any warning of one. Many of the young executives felt the steely fingers of panic, and debated calling their bosses. Others tried, but the phones were out. Cell phones, guaranteed to work in emergencies, were equally mute.

Security goons herded clients on the floor to a bar where drinks were on the house, although the ice supply was dubious. Some entertainers were roused and thrown into the breach, although their talents, without amplifiers, were questionable. The remaining ladies of the evening, enhanced by the dim candles, plied their trade. But to little avail. The elevators weren't working.

As the minutes ticked by, managers began to get reports, brought by puffing maintenance employees, that the high-rise hotels' water pumps had stopped. Now they had trouble.

The electrical industry was galvanized. All across the continent, control rooms had registered the outage . . . and the weaknesses of the system. Working ingenious engineering marvels, utilities folks got the national grid back up and pumping, but it took nine hours. Industry flacks quickly put out a story that the brownouts had been due to an operator's heart attack while performing a test at a major generating station.

Of course, the feds got involved right away, at various levels and in various guises—from FBI to Defense to Energy—and they came down hard on trade associations that had been delegated responsibility for Y2K and all-risk emergency preparedness. We trusted you guys! What went wrong? How could you let us down? How could it have happened? Sabotage? Are our systems really that poorly prepared—not so much for Y2K itself as for the domino effects?

CEOs, CIOs, even CFOs and their need-to-know underlings quickly learned the cause. The technospeak word they all used was *destabilize*. Destabilization gave them pause to think. They did their analyses of the damage that individual and simultaneous breakdowns of various magnitudes could cause; of possible alternate switching patterns to provide reduced power for vital services. And of course, they did bottom-line breakouts to mollify anxious shareholders. Destabilization of the national—even continental—electrical system could not be an issue. It had to be fixed. But *could* it be?

Even the medium-term scenarios were grim. Those who read the reports took to heart the lessons they contained. It was already too late to remediate the entire grid; they had poured hundreds of millions of dollars into making the systems compliant. All they could do now was create standby plans to cover demand and, in the event of trouble, plead with the public to cut usage until all systems were repaired—just like on a scorching summer's day, only more so.

Inevitably, hotshot reporters out to make their names started to dig behind the screen of official blandness. After a while, hard-nosed inquiries helped piece together a second explanation for the brownouts: No, it had not been a heart attack, but something more serious; there had been a major failure in a turbine at Boulder Dam. The story held for a while, then the young iconoclasts dug deeper. Eventually, one of the media people found the security guard who had been on duty that early morning. She promised the guard $25,000 to blow the whistle; he accepted $40,000 from the competition.

Authorities had immediately classified the story of Harold Bracken *Top Secret—Eyes Only*. And overnight Harold, who was being held pending arraignment on classified charges of sabotage, became a national hero—a guy who had dared to test the system to see how bad Y2K would be for the entire nation. His trial was postponed. Then under enormous public and political pressure, charges were dropped and Bracken was quietly released. He was reinstated with back pay and assigned to a make-work project. But never again was he invited to an office cookout.

Gstaad, Switzerland
Spring 1999

Before things really started to groove, the Russian Org had convoked a worldwide peace conference at Gstaad, in ever-neutral Switzerland. It had not bypassed the Papus' attention that the World Economic Conference took place in nearby Davos every winter, at which the CEOs of the mightiest multinational corporations held forth. Their get-together was likewise held off-season, because even in the hospitable Alps reservations were unavailable to unknowns, no matter how wealthy, during the snowy months. The Russian hosts chose to go with Gstaad because it was a class location.

It took a certain amount of gentle persuasion, verbal and otherwise, to gather the plenipotentiaries from around the world at the fabled resort. There the Papus' ministers, ambassadors, and consiglieri met their opposites from empires anchored in Tel Aviv, Lagos, Bogotá, Hong Kong, Macao, Bangkok, Las Vegas, and other American urbs for ten days of tense dealing and nine nights of extravagantly competitive orgying. Lucre, lust, and Lugers had come together in passionate as well as decadent display.

During the working sessions, the legates hammered out a peace treaty worthy of the secretary of state—advised, in part, by expert consultants suborned long before. Representatives formerly with the FBI and CIA, the Royal Canadian Mounted Police, Scotland Yard, la Sûreté National, the Bundeskriminalamt, Shin Bet, and others brought to the table impressive folders and manuals to bolster expert advice on countermeasures their previous employers might invoke to hinder the Papus' business dealings. True, a few consultants may have been playing both sides and informing official bodies about the conference, but it was hazardous short-term employment not favored by most professionals.

Under the Gstaad peace treaty, the mainland Chinese—working through Hong Kong—were granted special license to promote shortages in the vitamin, food supplement, health, and sex pill industries, but only with the proviso that the Russians could examine their books and that shipments were under Russian control. The Israelis came out with no special privileges, but were allowed to continue their profitable lines in weapons and electronics.

Drugs remained the province of the Colombians, but the Org also negotiated truce and no-fire zone agreements between the Cali emperors and representatives of the renegade general who ran the Golden Triangle of Southeast Asia and who—it was contemptuously alleged by Org ambassadors—still depended on the bumbling help of the highly ventilated CIA. The Mexicans, who had symbolic, partial-observer status at the conference, were assured that supply lines would continue to run through their country, but since they provided only support services that were at best erratic, they derived no tangible benefit from the meeting.

The Italians—those in Sicily and Reggio Calabria, as well as on Long Island—were told to stick strictly to gaming and prostitution. They were also strongly warned that any inclination to discuss Russian operations with the FBI would be forcibly and rapidly dealt with.

Back in the old country, the Org took advantage of Yeltsin's liquid preoccupations and of the general discombobulation of Russia to commandeer creaking Russian factories, sometimes by force, although often through the familial, high-profile bankers they had allowed to cash in on democracy. They refitted the plants with the latest machine tools from Germany; ordered the highest quality steel from Sweden, England, and Spain; and started to slipstream survival hardware on ultramodern roboticized production lines. Their production included knockoff Japanese generators, Buffalo Bill brand freeze-dried foods (complete with American content-and-nutrition information), Dolley Madison gourmet ready-to-eat meals, Maine Woods and Rodeo Drive camping gear, water and fuel containers by Saks Fifth Avenue and Nieman Marcus, water purifiers by Olay, even a handy line of long- and short-barreled guns for the enthusiasts' arsenals—exact replicas of Winchesters, Glocks, Kochs, and Berettas.

By summer 1999, the Papus' worldwide hegemony was firmly

established. The Russian Mafia was the undisputed master of the survival equipment business.

The New York Times carried a few brief reports of scattered illicit commercial activity, which the Org rather liked, since to them this critical acclaim seemed to be recognition that they had arrived. But hints that its paper supplies might dwindle discouraged the daily from tying the stories together into a major investigation. Without a lead from the *Times,* editors of other journals and the primary TV shockschlockzines did not realize anything untoward was afoot.

When it came time, the Papus of Brighton Beach had reckoned long before, some of their graduate smoothies would leak morsels of info to favored reporters. The resulting publicity would, they calculated, increase the squeeze on the American public by cycling up demand and playing on hysteria, and thus justify even more outrageous top-dollar prices. They rather favored giving news broadcaster Bart Branson an exclusive, because his debonair looks and manner reminded them of what they would like to be. But they couldn't leak—at least not yet.

Still, as profits flowed into Org-owned banks in Geneva and Zurich, Vaduz, Grand Cayman, Aruba, and Melanesia, there was major Slavic jollification in Brighton Beach. Short-lasted? Well, once the Bureau got itself untangled from hunting high-profile suspects in raccoon country and along railroad tracks, and making too many barrel-chested claims, it was almost too late. But the full force of law enforcement did eventually cut into the Org's monopoly, and the price of survival supplies once again dropped—although not to pre-Org comfort levels.

CHAPTER EIGHT

Los Padres National Forest
Spring 1999
To the north and east of Los Olivos, the second range of the Santa Ynez Mountains forms a barrier sheltering the Dick Smith Wilderness area of Los Padres National Forest, a huge preserve—3.75 million acres—of rugged, parched terrain. The forest is also a prime growing ground for entrepreneurial graduates of the California university system, especially those from the two schools that specialize in agriculture, UC Davis and Cal Poly. To some bemused taxpayers, the grads of these two institutions seem to go either into boutique viticulture and the wine trade or into high-tech marijuana growing. The latter tend to favor covert growing on government property, deep in near-inaccessible ravines and canyons. Using nature's own camouflage, the pot farmers artfully interweave their plants in these innocent forests, concealing their crops from all but the closest scrutiny by armed state and federal helicopter task forces.

Once, a county agriculture commissioner in the northwestern

quadrant of the state included pot—the state's largest cash crop—in his annual report. The board of supervisors paled collectively; the report was withdrawn; and a revised version speedily issued.

Little of the back country is given over to the California version of the old Appalachian moonshine game. Elsewhere, people who treasure the solitude hike and ride in awe of nature's rugged majesty. Here and there, back-country explorers have found sites obviously sacred to centuries of bygone Chumash Indians. A very few California condors, released into the Sespe Wilderness in the hope that they will survive and breed, soar majestically overhead—and all too often crash, after falling prey to some appurtenance of civilized man.

A few humans, also, live in the vastness—legally and illegally. A scattering of them dwell there legally, in harmony with the vastness and far beyond the reach of census takers. Then there are the runaways, some of whom find it inconvenient to linger where law enforcement may stumble onto them. Others bear deep resentments against authority in any form, their anger tracing back to the 1960s and early 1970s. They prefer the challenge of making it on their own, away from what they see as a corrupt, luxury-driven, prying society.

Increasingly, the forest has sheltered a different breed of dropout. Where survivalists of the 1970s feared environmental cataclysm and espoused the communal, natural life, today's refugees are not so much into the development of low-tech sustainability. They are either—like the Steinharts—fervent fundamentalist Christians, convinced that Armageddon is upon us, or computer geeks who for different reasons have come to somewhat the same conclusion and want to ride out the dawn of the new millennium close to Mother Nature, away from the machines they helped to program.

By summer 1998, a fair sprinkling of highly skilled computer programmers decided that Y2K would make life in population centers unlivable. They made hard-line preparations for life in the outback, without fanfare. Early on, they coined an acronym for the new Armageddon, TEOTWAWKI—The End of the World As We Know It—and flooded friendly Internet sites with dire warnings. The new backwoodsmen were not all longhairs, but often close-cropped, left-brained cybernerds.

In spring 1999, a scattered few of them headed north, through Santa Barbara and over San Marcos Pass. Some came south, turning eastward near Buellton and moving inland. They were mostly men—some from as far north as Silicon Valley or Sacramento, some from San Francisco—migrating south in hopes of more clement weather. Women came, too—some on their own, some in couples. All passed through the Santa Ynez Valley and disappeared into the vastness of Los Padres National Forest. There they established individual encampments far enough apart to give them turf, near enough to be sociable on occasion and to help one another should the need arise.

The new arrivals found traces of other inhabitants among the California pine and oak. At first they made contact gingerly, wary about having their space invaded, yet eager to see if others were on the same wavelength, or perhaps in possession of some good grass. After the new arrivals and their predecessors had snuffled each other out, the straggling encampments—which were more like a series of outposts strung together by bush telegraph—split into three loose circuits.

The Christians tried to stay as far away from planters and plantations as possible, and they kept their camps austere and as impeccable as conditions permitted. They got their sermons over the radio; some had battery-operated TVs.

The high-tech refugees were of much the same mind-set as the pot growers, so the two groups got along fairly well. But the newcomers also kept a discreet distance, since they had no desire to get busted and face mandatory sentencing for illicit agriculture. The ex-nerds were latter-day hippies, sure, but more. Many of them had come to the mountains the same way the Steinharts had—via universities or high-pressure electronics jobs.

The computer guys were loners, not desperadoes. Exercising their all-American, God-given right to live a life of hardship, they didn't like to be interfered with or pestered. Indeed, down in the Valley some of them muttered about resisting intrusion. They were, however, camping on the people's land, as were the other illegal residents. One big problem for everybody was staying clear of the law. They had all heard on the sylvan grapevine that the US Forest Service, under fire from many quarters for playing footsie with the lumbering industry, was looking to score brownie points by not only charging day-users of the forest but also ferreting out illegal campers and trying them for trespass. Their other problem was having to hump in supplies.

Whatever their reasons and differences, all these basically self-disenfranchised individuals shared a common view that they did not, could not, fit in with the greater majority of Americans and were better off isolated. Thus, to varying degrees they mistrusted, suspected, and even feared those forces of an ever more violent culture careening toward the mystery of the millennium.

The activities of the DEA and US Forest Service were commonly held as proof positive that the government was potentially capable of true menace; if small groups of armed officials, whatever their acronyms, and a few helicopters occasionally intruded in pursuit of pot growers—a pursuit even the most benign of forest dwellers viewed as specious—then what was to prevent larger groups of armed officials, from the Army or National Guard, and dozens, if not hundreds, of helicopters from descending upon them for reasons equally specious?

This logic, however skewed, was fueled by extremists who smoldered with hatred for any government intervention by force of arms. Beginning with Kent State, they could, and did, recite numerous examples—the revelations of Waco began the most recent. Many openly viewed the bombing of the federal building in Oklahoma City as an act of justice. Armed defense, they argued, was the only defense against the armed invasion that would inevitably come. All that was needed was another excuse; and more and more, as the remaining days of 1999 dwindled down, they saw Y2K as not only the perfect excuse but the beginning of Armageddon.

They were, they believed, prepared.

* * *

Among the newcomers was Fred Georgeson, with a PhD in electrical engineering—a once-acerbic, wispy nerd with dropout tendencies. He had long cursed his family name, Djordjevic, which stuttered so cumbrously across American tongues. As soon as he was legally able, he changed his name to a more palatable, anglicized version.

But he had been unable, throughout his thirty-seven years, to shake a combination of guilt and anger that still clutched him to the bosom of his past. Computers, in which Fred had immersed himself in hopes of escaping the perplexing personality that ruled him, had provided no answers. Nor had therapists or psychiatrists. He had spent short spells in mental wards, some of them on suicide watch, and had consumed more lithium than he could remember. Still, the frustration, the blackness of despair had at times welled up and overcome him. And also, he had had to battle a cancer that gnawed at him during his last years in Silicon Valley.

Fred bitterly knew that neither his academic distinctions nor his later electronic prosperity overrode the fact that he looked too much like a caricature of a mangy Balkan bomber. He had long since become used to barely concealed stares at his homeliness, but they hurt more when he came down from the mountain fastness to deal with civilization.

Fred had come to the western slope of the Los Padres circuitously. Like the Steinharts, he had upped stakes from Silicon Valley, but for a different combination of reasons. A major cause for his departure from civilization, and from a job that paid over $150,000, was fatigue, and then burnout.

In 1996, he learned he had cancer. He did chemotherapy and radiation, but in mid-1998, Fred's doctors told him he was terminal. Oddly, it was almost a relief. He still looked strong and felt pretty good. He had more money than he needed. If he was going to die, he reckoned, he didn't want to be among a bunch of panicky high-rollers in the nation's most plasticized garden-spot. Coming on top of his battles with depression, and the hospitalizations they had brought, he saw that civilization just didn't hack it for him anymore. So he resigned; changed his money into wads of traveler's checks, since he didn't trust ATMs; and headed out to the Los Padres.

While in the wilds, he had let his hair grow back out till it reached nearly below his shoulder blades, although he kept it bunched up in a major ponytail, as a token of conformity, when he came down to town. Fred was tall and slouchy and shaggy. He reminded some of a split rail. His face was memorable for its bumps and pits, and he tended to avoid eye contact except in direct conversation. He could talk with the best of them—and did, in a high-pitched voice that sounded sometimes argumentative—in the saloons of Santa Ynez and Los Olivos. His chosen topic of conversation, however, was not everyone's favorite: he obsessively wanted to warn people about Y2K. Faced with smug indifference, even hostility, he had convinced himself, as had many of his fellow tribesmen, that they had definitely made the right decision in heading into the outback.

Fred had a neat little spread, about an hour by unpaved road into the forest, pleasantly temperate in summer and not all that bad in winter. He had to be wary of his fire, not only because of the smoke but because of the forest. He had been rattled once or twice upon hearing the echo of distant rifle fire, then got accustomed to the rounds fired off by pot growers farther back in the hill country. Nowadays, the fed-state task forces used infrared to scope the plants, because the growers had learned some concealment tricks, too.

Because of its relative calm and beauty, Fred thought of his site as a sort of therapeutic oasis, a place where maybe he could work out the knots and writhings that had landed him in hospital rubber-rooms as well as in radiation therapy chambers. He had long cast himself as bitter. Bitter about the cancer—even if it now seemed to be in remission. Bitter about his unresolved dual-track heritage and his anachronistic birth-religion. Bitter about the inhumane demands the job had made on him, and what it had cost him, including, perhaps, his health. Bitter about his part in the high-tech revolution. Bitter about advertising and the media, for making light of serious questions and emphasizing only the glossy life. Bitter about the demands and expectations of society. Bitter, because his lumpy face and long locks made him less than a good American . . .

On a cool, sunny Sunday afternoon, Fred Georgeson found himself behind the wheel of an open Chevy truck that had been haphazardly spray-painted dusty brown and pale green in a camouflage pattern. Some fifteen men had piled into the back. In the passenger seat was the owner of the truck, who wore an OD T-shirt and camouflage pants; his first name was Dean, and Fred had already forgotten his last name.

Dean was instructing Fred on the idiosyncrasies of his truck to make sure he was comfortable with it. They were going for a "test drive"—a dozen or so miles over unpaved roads and then about twenty on paved. That was it.

"Just so you get used to the weight," Dean said. "All the guys in the back. Just a Sunday drive. Good of you to volunteer, man."

"No problem." Fred was busy watching the contours of the narrow forest road. He could feel the extra weight in back, and supreme concentration was required to keep the truck from lurching, and to adjust to using the manual transmission.

"We're in good shape now," Dean said. "All our vehicles have second drivers like you, so we're ready for anything."

Fred was hazy about what "anything" might be, but it sounded good. He'd volunteered to be a standby driver at the last meeting of the big, loose bunch of people who lived in his area. The idea was to maintain an emergency plan in the event of fire, so that vehicles were organized enough to get everybody out. Or, as they'd announced at the meeting, if something connected to Y2K came up. The "fleet" was also called up once in a while to transport large quantities of supplies. Other drivers had mentioned gasoline and water—and heavy cases of they-didn't-know-what.

Fred knew what, but he didn't give a crap. He also knew that Dean was part of the militia group, who kept what they were doing pretty much under their hats. He didn't give a crap about that either.

It wasn't a bad thing to have somebody paying attention to fire evacuation, and providing security if it was needed. Everybody knew there were weapons someplace, but other than occasional practice-firing Fred had heard about, it was no big deal. He was happy to do his small part, as any volunteer fireman would be.

"So," Dean said briskly, "what do you think will happen?"

"Happen?"

"At the end of the year—Y2K, man."

"Not much," Fred said. "At least not up here."

"And if it did?"

"Got all we need, don't we? Nobody's going to come up here . . . Down in the Valley, out there, like I've been telling everybody, it could go to hell in a handbasket. Nobody listens."

"Right!" Dean seemed enthusiastic. "But *we* gotta care. What happens if *we* run out of stuff? What if things out there are screwed up for months, man, and we run out of food and we can't get more? What if the DEA or FBI or the fuckin' Army takes control of distribution—or comes looking for us?"

Fred glanced over at Dean, who was gazing out ahead and pulling on a cigarette. Dean didn't look like one of the crazies; on the contrary, he looked like he had it together—short hair, clean shaven, trim, alert.

"What if . . . ," Fred echoed. "If things get screwed up, they probably won't have time to worry about us." The truth is, all this talk was confusing. It bothered him because he, unlike Dean, could not fix on a scenario that made sense. When he tried to think about the end of the year, it made him so nervous he couldn't function.

"But," Dean said, after a pause, "you've got to agree that preparation helps. All the women, the kids. We have to be prepared, man. We *are* prepared."

"Right. Good." Fred was glad to hear this. Glad that *some*body was paying attention to future arrangements. Glad too that he himself was part of the plan. No one down in the Valley ever listened when *he* talked about being prepared. He wished Dean would shut up.

"You know, don't you," Dean said, "that Uncle Sammy hasn't

done jack-shit. You know, don't you, that if things really do break loose, they have no plan. All they can do is call out the troops if the balloon goes up."

Fred especially didn't want to hear this. It made him even more nervous. He needed to concentrate on his driving; already he'd gotten too close to low tree branches, setting off howls and curses from the men in back.

"They're doing their best," he said, lamely. "To get ready."

"Yeah," Dean came back. "Doing their best to get the fuckin' *banks* ready, and big business. Oil and transportation, *maybe*. Utilities, *maybe*. Food and water, *maybe*. The fat cats will be okay no matter what. You can be sure about that. But the rest of the peasants will get the usual hind tit—especially us. The feds don't like us, man. Just like Waco. We're freaks, dangerous, man. Things go bad, the feds will control everything: food, water, utilities. We'll get squat, *nada,* zero, zip. They won't care if we starve, believe it. So *then* where are we?"

Fred shrugged. He knew where this was leading; he'd heard it a thousand times. But all he had to do was drive. And stay cool.

"I'll tell you where we'll be," Dean continued. "We'll be strong enough to take what we need if we have to. And we'll be strong enough to defend ourselves if anybody comes up here after us."

"Okay." Fred nodded agreeably. "Right, man."

"You on the Net? You have a computer?"

"Not anymore." Fred smiled at himself. "Been there, done that."

"You know about Canada's Y2K plan?"

"Not a thing."

"You should. They've got *their* shit together in a tight sock. Imagine, Canada. They've got a complete plan. It's on the Internet. You can learn about the whole thing with a tap of the keys. It's called Operation Abacus. They're ready, man. All navy vessels in port, or on close coastal patrol, by end of year. All military services on duty from Christmas through New Year's; no leaves. All critical services and utilities employees, same thing; no holidays. And on and on . . . while we've got squat, *nada,* zero, zip. Think on it."

Fred did not want to think on it; nor was he sure he believed it. Anyway, he still didn't give a crap. It made him even more confused, and angry. "Swell" was all he could say.

"You don't have to believe me," Dean said. "Get on the Net and look it up. I'll give you the address. Now, why do you think you haven't heard about Canada? Why do you think it hasn't been in the papers or on TV? Because *we* don't have a plan. The only *plan* the feds have is to call out the troops."

"Okay, okay. Look, I hear you. But if there isn't any plan, then it's too late anyway, isn't it? At least it's too late to do anything about it in—what, six weeks?"

"Right!" Dean smacked his fist on the dashboard. "Absolutely right! Which is why we need to be ready. Which is why we *are* ready."

"Good. Glad to hear it."

"Which also is why you need to be ready—why we're taking this little drive. Something comes up, we can move."

"Good," Fred said again. "Glad to know that. Why the camouflage paint?"

"Helicopters."

"Got it." Fred processed this for a few seconds before he began to feel suspicious, confused, and a little fearful. They were coming to the blacktop now; he could see the clearing ahead. He geared down early and their dust flew about them. Dean was checking his road map.

"Okay," he said. "Hang a left. Stay about five miles under the limit and we'll cruise for a while. Nothing to it." He lit up another cigarette. "Man, we are *ready*."

Buellton, California
November 1999
The First County National Bank and Trust Company of Buellton, California, had evolved from three earlier financial institutions that dated back to the late nineteenth century. Depression, wild inflation, drought, flooding, earthquake, pests, and other works of man and

nature had brought on amalgamations in the Santa Ynez Valley, as elsewhere, but the FCNB&T was one of the few locally owned banks to survive in the face of vast pressure from statewide, even nationwide, competition. It was a proud little institution in a weathered, two-story red brick building at the corner of Avenue of the Flags and Ronald Reagan Drive, right at the center of Old Buellton.

Inside the aging yet newly renovated structure, the officers were as up-to-date as their Harvard and Wharton B-School degrees and the *Wall Street Journal* could make them. Above and beyond the demands of federal regulators, even snap inspections, the bank's management committee of three worried in advance about its responsibilities to its largely rural ranching and farming and small-business clientele when Y2K struck. They decided to run a test of their remediated system. Analysis of their records showed demand for computer services was at its lowest from 2:00 to 4:00 Sunday mornings, so they scheduled their test for the Saturday night and Sunday after Thanksgiving.

The computer systems manager set up for his night-long siege of retesting. Meanwhile, Vice President Henry Kirsted, on the first shift, slouched at his desk with a thermos of coffee as well as Virginia smoked ham and aged cheddar cheese with chutney sandwiches on his wife's homemade sourdough bread, and figured he would catch up on some reading. Four hours; he might just finish the Tom Clancy he had started on his last business trip East.

Shortly after 3:00 A.M., a man ambled up to the ATM and tried to push his card into the slot. It was refused. He punched the keyboard and kicked the wall, swearing copiously until Henry and the night security guard came out.

"Can't get nothin' out of your damn money machine. Need a drink . . . and some food. Can't get no foldin' money. What's up?"

Henry soothed, "Happy to take care of you, sir. How much do you need?"

"Hunderd will do me."

"If you'll give me your driver's license and card—and wait right here, sir—I'll get your cash inside."

"OK, if that's the best you can do." When Henry had disappeared, the driver unzipped his fly, then swayed over to the wall. "Hell of a way to run a bank," he muttered. "Playing midnight teller."

The bank had made provision for just such an event. One hundred was a lot from the cash reserve, but they should still be OK. Henry noted the man's particulars and his card number, then went outside and gave him the cash.

"You look pretty tired. Maybe you could pull in at one of our motels," Henry suggested.

"Hell no! Headin' down the highway. Got me a nice little lady lined up, too."

"OK." Henry shrugged. "There's a rest stop about ten miles east, in case you decide to stop."

The man grunted and staggered off.

Henry resumed his reading. The elderly guard, unhappy about having to share his watch, tried to look alert but was having obvious difficulty staying awake. Henry glanced up from his book and grinned. "It's OK, Elmer. I don't need company. Go ahead, hit the sack."

Between 4:00 and 5:30 A.M., two more people came by for money—a surprise to Henry and the guard. When Jack Wheelock, the bank president, took over the watch at 6:00 A.M., the cash reserve was down to $240 of the original $500 they had figured would last till the end of the test period.

Jack had two customers—at 8:37 and 9:12, respectively. Together, they took $165. Jack smiled. No problem with his explanation that the machine was being repaired. On the contrary, the customers thanked him for being there rather than just hanging out a sign directing them to the nearest big bank branch.

At 9:43, Bob Greensmith, one of the area's major ranchers, pulled up in his shiny Chrysler. Jack was outside doing stretches in the early morning sun before heat blanketed the Valley. They greeted each other warmly. "On your way to church, Bob? Sorry I'm going to miss out today. Gotta pull sentry duty here—our ATM's down. Need some cash?"

"Yeah. We're going on down to LA. Give me a couple hundred on my check card?"

"Why . . . sure!" Jack swallowed. "Be right back."

The bank president hastened into the hall, took the remaining cash from the reserve drawer, dug into his own pockets, and came up with a total of $120. He winced, then went back outside.

"Hey, Bob. Sorry, but you've run us straight out of cash. Hope this'll be enough till you get to another machine. Real sorry, but you know how it is with these dang computers."

Greensmith studied him for a moment. "Anything you're not telling me, Jack? You don't look very happy."

"Well, no . . . I'm not. It's no fun being unable to serve a valued customer like you."

"Cut the bullshit, Jack. What's going on? Why're *you* here, instead of one of the tellers? The bank got troubles?"

"Well, no. Just routine." It was lame, Jack knew. "We just didn't want to ask them to come in on a Saturday night and all." Wheelock backed-and-filled. "No, no problems. None at all. Just making some computer repairs, is all. Monday everything'll be hunky-dory again."

Internally, the bank president kicked himself. He was aware his weak answers might have raised more doubts in Greensmith's mind.

The bronzed rancher folded the bills carefully into his whipcords and climbed into the deep seat of the Chrysler. "I sure hope you're not spinnin' me, Wheelock. Wouldn't want a nice long business relationship to go sour."

Jack felt drained as he watched the Chrysler purr away. He was not reassured to see Greensmith talking into his cell phone as he rounded the corner and disappeared.

Inside, the bank techie sweated and strained, and at 10:00 A.M. he reported to Wheelock. "I'm not going to make it, Jack. The remediation has created more problems. Trouble is, I can't restore the system right away. We'll have to direct people to other banks till I can get it all online again."

Jack Wheelock groaned, nodding. Instinct told him to prepare for the worst.

Word spread through Buellton and other Valley communities. By noon, what had started as a trickle of people at the ATM machine became a stream—the makings of a run on the First County National Bank and Trust. Then just after 12:30, the live truck from KSQK arrived, followed by Gerri LaPorte in her new VW Beetle. Jack, the watchman, and the techie stayed behind locked doors, peering out through lowered blinds as the crowd swelled. Jack had thought about summoning the bank staff, but realized there was nothing they could do.

The temperature in the flat, enclosed Valley rose. Customers beat on the doors and windows, screamed about the FDIC, demanded cash. Wheelock called both the police department in Buellton and the nearby sheriff's station to ask for a control presence. Phones rang off the hook—no longer inquisitive local calls, but voices from Chicago and New York, then London, Frankfurt, even Hong Kong, where it was already Monday.

Around 2:00 P.M., a helicopter clacked in, dropping off grim-faced men and women who had "Government" stamped on their furrowed foreheads. Heavy metal suitcases were chained to their wrists. After a quick conference behind locked doors, the feds stepped out into the crowd. They explained through a bullhorn that they were representatives of the FDIC, the FBI, and the Secret Service.

The FDIC woman promised that all depositors would get their money, but pleaded that they not try to withdraw it all immediately. "The federal government *guarantees* that your money is safe—*all* of it! If the police will help you form an orderly line, we'll take care of your immediate needs, but we ask you to settle down. Your accounts are OK. Please believe us."

The crowd calmed a bit. Judging from the muttering on the rim, however, many were still wary. By then, the story was out: A bank that had sought to run a Y2K compliance test on its own system had crashed. Depositors were unable to access their money.

Helen Hope came off her Exercycle and bustled into the kitchen. For the hundredth time she thanked her lucky stars she made enough money at the radio station to have sprung for a new oven. It had been hell bending over the old one, especially when she was wearing the hot pants Don demanded on her days off.

She opened the door and sniffed, poking a sliver of wood into the chocolate marble cakes. Almost done. Grandma's recipes still worked, even if they took time. So much more delish than those premixes.

She smiled and bopped to the 1970s oldies on the radio, glanced in the mirror, adjusted her frosted-gold hair, checked her Everglo lipstick, wheeled on her froufrou pink slippers to check the rear view, and shivered with a frisson of lust as she glanced in her full-length, gilt kitchen mirror at the slight overhangs. Not bad for fifty-four going on thirty-eight. Don's far-out fantasies kept her young.

Sundays, except for mandatory promo and fund-raiser appearances, were sacred to baking in preparation for the new retirement venture "Hot Stuff Bakes by Helen Hope." And of course, Sundays were when Don liked to indulge his latest whims—after golf.

The phone rang. It was a very scattered intern, holding down the deserted newsroom. "Miz Hope—uh—Helen, this is Tracey at the station. They told me to tell you to, uh, quote, get your Christian ass in here, like now. End quote."

"What's up?"

"Looks like there's a run on the County Bank and Trust. Live truck's on its way now. Gerri's meeting it there. Big stuff. They want you in here ASAP!"

"Tell Mort to hold twenty. My cakes are in the oven; he'll understand. But a run on the bank? What's that? Jack Wheelock having some kind of special promotion—on a Sunday, when he should be in church? They didn't notify us about it! I keep telling them they need a PR person, bad."

"No, ma'am. Yes. Please, ma'am, just come here quick. It's getting crazy, and no one's in yet. I'll tell Mort about your cakes."

"Tell him I'm on my way."

Helen willed the oven to bake quicker, then went to reinforce her makeup and to apply special moisturizer to her neck. Despite everything she did, the wrinkles always showed up on camera. Too embarrassing. She threw a light blazer over the Frederick's of Hollywood angora tank-top. A hint of boob was OK on camera. Couldn't go overboard in Buellton and the surrounding landscape. Too late to change, anyway.

By the time her emergency preparations were done, the cakes were ready. Scrunching all her parts, Helen Hope eased into the Lexus LX 470-V8 and dusted down the county highway, onto the state road, thence briefly onto 101 and the turnoff leading to the squat cinderblock structure that was home to KSQK—"The Eyes and Ears of the Santa Ynez Valley."

She clacked into the newsroom, teeth aglow as always. Tracey and a couple of techies glanced up, then returned to their work. Helen paused at the sign screwed into the partition wall:

> THE FACT THAT YOUR VOICE IS AMPLIFIED TO THE DEGREE WHERE IT REACHES FROM ONE END OF THE COUNTRY TO THE OTHER DOES NOT CONFER UPON YOU GREATER WISDOM OR UNDERSTANDING THAN YOU POSSESSED WHEN YOUR VOICE REACHED ONLY FROM ONE END OF THE BAR TO THE OTHER.
> —EDWARD R. MURROW, 1965

As usual, she snorted and shook her head. Helen Hope had never had a drinking problem.

Mort filled her in as she sashayed onto the set. "Gerri's coming up in about five," he said, looking harried. "Someone say you don't know what a run on a bank is?"

"No, sounds like a good stunt. I mean, why all the fuss and bother? If my cakes are ruined, I'll sue you."

"No, sugar, this is serious. A run on a bank is when everyone wants their money out. Right now. See?"

"Why would they do that?"

"Because something has gone wrong. I think I know what it is, but I don't want to speculate. We're already flying by the seat of our pants."

"Oooh, sounds exciting!"

Mort looked at his anchor with distaste mingled with admiration. "You never change, do you?"

"So what do you want me to do? And where's that asshole, my ever-loving coanchor?"

"Lewis? He's at a Little League game. Actually, he asked if he should come in his baseball uniform. I told him not to hurry. We'll cue you with cards, you'll have the prompter rolling, and I'll talk you through it. Stay real loose. Got it?"

"OK, whatever. I can run with it without Lewis. He wouldn't understand anyway, would he? But hey, *my* money's in there, too. Should I tell Don to go over? He's playing golf."

"No time for that. Here comes Gerri."

Mort raced from the set to the control room. The burly floor manager signaled with his fingers: *five . . . four . . . three . . . two . . . one.*

"Hey there! This is Helen Hope at KSQK. Well, *wow!* Do *we* have *breaking news* for *you!* Big things happening right here in little old Buellton, and we're going to begin our team coverage right now with a live report from our own Gerri LaPorte . . . Gerri?"

The livecam panned to the crowd outside the bank, where blue-uniformed police and now khaki-clad sheriffs were trying to push the crowd away. They were losing the struggle. People continued to pound on the glass doors of the bank building. The microphones picked up a ragged chant: "We *want* our *money, now!*" Someone threw a rock at the bank of ATM machines.

Gerri's voice could hardly be heard from the edge of the melee. Mort cut to the live truck's mastcam and rotated it to catch sight of vehicles coming into the center of town as the director spoke softly but firmly into her earpiece. "Helen, network just called on the redline. We're going live, nationwide, in two minutes. I'll pull back from

Gerri. Make an intro. Remember, you're talking to the entire United States. Hell, maybe to the world."

Helen reached under the desk to tug her hot pants loose from her crotch, then squiggled to rearrange her cheeks in the straightback chair. She touched her stiff, unyielding hair; gave her neck a quick massage; fastened the professional smile over her full set of crowns; and took a deep, nearly giddy breath.

"Good afternoon from the Santa Ynez Valley in Central California. About an hour ago . . ." As she listened to Mort's slow dictation and talked, the livecam swept the scene in front of the bank. The police were now reinforced by officers in riot-and-combat gear. They looked young, scared. Biting their lips. Trying to appear authoritative.

Sheriff Mike Propoulos was demanding dispersal. The camera caught his look of concern as he heard the same noise the mikes picked up—the sound of popping. People hit the ground.

Gerri's voice screamed off-camera, *"I hear gunfire . . ."*

The last anyone saw of the broadcast came as the handheld livecam zeroed in on a knot of people trying to pry the bars off a side window. At that point, the coast-to-coast network's satellite vibrated intensely and its signal began to fail, whereupon Helen Hope lost it, into an open mike: "Well, I'll be goddamned!"

Then KSQK went dead.

CHAPTER NINE

Santa Barbara, California
November 1999
The California National Guard, with its pay and retirement bennies, was a good deal for people who liked to play soldier. There were weekly evening meetings, not too strenuous; some weekends away from the wife and kids; a couple of spring or summer weeks in the boonies. Depending on your specialty, you didn't even have to stay in great shape.

But Y2K changed all that. The Santa Barbara unit, designated the 376th Field Artillery Battery, was deactivated during the military budget cuts of 1995, and was attached, officially but moribund, to a more energetic command of military police in Oxnard, near the big Navy installations on the coast. By spring of 1999, things had altered more rapidly than anyone who ever wore a uniform could have imagined. Santa Barbara's weekend militarists were reactivated and held on the table of organization, in a transmogrification that bewildered even the most ardent student of the military mind, as the 128th

Quartermaster Company—Light Airdrop Supply. Headquarters got spiffed up; all stones anywhere near the parade ground were painted quartermaster red. Men and women who had been indolently collecting benefits and pay were sternly reminded of their obligations.

It had been a long time since the unit's members—officers or enlisted—had fired anything bigger than a Fourth of July firecracker. Their first weekend retraining session, in November 1999, was on the firing range at Camp Roberts, 107 coccyx-jolting, convoy-crawling miles up Highway 101 aboard belching GI trucks. The last of the thirty-year men from Nam, guys who had been in Desert Storm, and new recruits fresh out of high school all fired for record at the large bull's-eyes over the pits until they qualified, no matter how long it took. Old-fashioned, hard-nosed Regular Army Drill Instructors roared profanely that raising "Maggie's Drawers," the time-honored red flag of dismal failure to hit the target, showed unacceptable incompetence, and worse. Officers, sensibly, fired separately and later.

The 128th jolted back into the Santa Barbara Armory on a Monday as the sun crawled up over the ocean at Ventura. They arrived home just in time to shower and get to their day jobs.

The reinvigorated National Guard had a new mission: civil disorder training. Late-model six-by-sixes and Humvees started to arrive at the military compound. Many of the trucks contained cartons of riot gear: body shields, clear face visors, vests, batons, and tear gas canisters. On Highway 101, blue-and-white signs appeared saying National Guard, with an arrow below indicating the proper turnoff.

The week after Camp Roberts, terse orders appeared on the unit's bulletin board:

<u>OPERATION CANYON CLINCHER</u>
<u>26–29 DECEMBER 1999</u>
MISSION: RECONNOITER MOUNTAINOUS TERRAIN AND CANYONS—LIAISON US FOREST SERVICE—LOS PADRES NATIONAL FOREST. (GRID COORDINATES TO FOLLOW.)

TRAINING MANEUVERS AROUND SB. COUNTY LAKE CACHUMA CAMPGROUND. RIOT CONTROL EXERCISES. PREPARE TO NEUTRALIZE HOSTILE ELEMENTS IF NECESSARY.

Gentlemen and grunts read the orders and went ballistic over losing part of their Christmas holiday. Then, grumbling among themselves, they debated the likelihood of having to confront fellow citizens if said "civil disorder" occurred, and theorized about various meanings of the term "hostile elements." A reserve major, Dick McGuinn, requested permission to discuss the orders with the unit commanding officer, a Regular Army lieutenant colonel who was ending an undistinguished career in a cushy berth. Major McGuinn came away only slightly less disturbed than he had gone in. He then called a meeting of his citizen soldiers at his house, and laid out the details. He added that, in the event of an emergency, the Santa Barbara unit could be transported to a disturbance up to 100 miles from home.

New York City
November 1999
Inside a windowless modern brick building in the West Fifties, editors hunched at their terminals in the large, designed-for-high-visual-impact network newsroom. In the tank Bart Branson, anchor of *Day's News*, with tie askew and shirt crumpled—not the crisp, London-stitched one he would soon wear on the air—slumped at the head of the oval table. Next to him slouched Herb Friedkin, head of the News Division and a hardened old-style newsman brought in to boost ratings after the network had fallen into third place because it had dipped too fervently into lifestyle reportage. Gradations of advertising, PR, promotion, opinion survey, and marketing minions formed a learning curve of power and intrigue along the delicate bends of the table en route to the far end where, neatly threaded and modishly tied, sat the president of Network News, a lawyer with a minor in showbiz.

The atmosphere in the room was almost incendiary. The anchor was expostulating in angry tones, far different from the mellifluous lilt with which he wooed his millions of viewers. "Look, we have a responsibility to our viewers—hell, even to the nation, if you will—and not least to ourselves. This is *hard news*. It's potential dynamite, I grant you. But that does not mean we overplay it. We run it as a straight story, down in the body of the cast." Bart's speech slipped back to the Milwaukee inner city of his childhood. "If there's another one, we handle it the same. We *don't* fucking sensationalize. We play it straight, and responsible."

Down the table, the president looked distinctly detached. He glanced at his watch, drummed his fingers. He could not be late for the national advertisers' cocktail reception upstairs. He fiddled with the gold cufflink he had fraternally removed from his shirt so he could roll up his sleeves.

"You overlook the major responsibility we have to the CEO," he sneered loftily, "and to the board, and to our stockholders." The last with only a brief hallowed intake of breath. "Do I need to remind you, Bart, that we are down to number three in the book?"

Herb, whose true baby was *Day's News,* shambled into the fray. He was a slight, permagray man whose facial rills complemented those in his shirt. His rasplike voice was famous in the news business—the trademark of one of the few survivors of the Murrow-friendly school of broadcast journalism.

"We've had this argument umpteen times. During and since Nam. Journalistic ethics versus corporate profit. I'm sick of it. You guys upstairs, all you think of is what the ticker says. But the ticker doesn't judge our performance, our moral honesty, the responsibilities of the journalist . . ."

"Herb, as you say, we've been down this road countless times," the president responded smoothly. "I feel your pain, but dammit, *get real!* We're in the entertainment business. Your ethics do you proud, yet this is nineteen ninety-nine. Wake up, guys. Get with the program! We're selling advertising. We do what it takes. Understood? Do I have to remind you again who pays your handsome salaries?" He paused for a moment. "I didn't want to do it this way, but I'm authorized by PJ. This is how we play Buellton: instant *now* leads with the California bank story. They've just about got it packaged. Rolling on the satellite in . . . thirteen minutes. *Day's News* leads this evening with a tamer, more sedate version.

"Polly Stone is already airborne in the production jet. She'll find a cornfield to land in. Her piece will lead *Nightscape* and she'll do *Morning Now* live from the field, maybe from an outhouse, or a jail cell, or wherever the panic takes her."

All heads turned to the other end of the table. The silence tried the limits of the in-house weapons-of-mass-destruction treaty. After a whoosh of exhaling, first Bart, then Herb folded.

Herb spoke for the losers. "Well, shit . . . you win. Rather's on his way out there. Brokaw's holding steady. Jennings is hanging loose. Doesn't give us much wiggle room, does it? Be nice just to have a major, clean-cut crime story, wouldn't it?"

Bart muttered, not quite to himself, "Yeah, but there's always *Compass*." The editorial side of the table smiled with happy vindication.

Jim Martin flicked the TV on to *Compass*, the program that followed *Nightscape*.

The network had had to fill the postmidnight slot with something. When presented with a novel proposal, the net bosses shrugged an indifferent OK, and soon found themselves ogling a high-maintenance audience of PBS after-hours intelligentsia, whereupon the spinmeisters sought to burnish the net's schlocky image by claiming the literate high ground. Since the viewers were happy and the show was dirt cheap to produce, network didn't interfere much with the individualistic way Si Aronowitz and his production team ran *Compass*—which was loose.

Si was a boomers' counterculture icon, the antithesis of media chic. One of his most trenchant qualities was his seemingly effortless ability to take the pulse of his audience. That, and the fact that he never talked down to people. He used his deep, cuddling voice to chat with his viewers, musing out loud, inviting them into his prodigious mind.

Tonight he smiled his usual timeworn smile of shared intelligence as he meandered through the opening monologue. "You can remind people to beware the source till you're blue in the face. But if it's been on TV, the story develops a life and a veracity of its own. Advertising and PR people have long known this truth. And now, once again"—he paused to give the camera his famous bloodhound look—"it's coming home to us, here on the editorial side, with a vengeance. The first waves of Y2K panic are gnawing visibly at the national psyche. Tides of overbuying roll through superstores, and yesterday we had yet another run on a bank in California. Lucky no one was seriously hurt."

Si shifted his position, consciously mimicking the guy in the suppository ads, and squinted past the camera. "There's talk—mind you, it's only unfounded gossip—that some of the shortages may have been artificially created. That there may actually be a criminal element at work here. We can't confirm this. But you heard it here first.

"Y2K has become the event that's too big for us any of us to comprehend. Part of the mix is that we who make up this broad and speckled land like to defy the punditry of those who sit around small tables and spit at each other on camera—because we like to think on our own."

He paused, drank from his trademark Styrofoam cup, and meandered on. "After the sixties and seventies, we started to make real money. We scrambled to be sharper images of ourselves, and we misplaced some of our truths along the way. One of these is what I call good old common sense. To get that common sense back, we've got to be honest with ourselves.

"Bear with me as I ramble—this subject got me thinking. Anyway, happily, we have never really *lost* our common sense, regardless of considerable evidence to the contrary. And now, lo and behold, along comes the Y2K Bug. We decide that no one really has a rat's ass of an idea what is going to happen. And we know damn well from previous experiences three decades ago, and also just a few painful months back, that no one in Washington is capable of telling the truth for longer than two seconds. With Y2K coming on top of the impeachment fiasco, we know, more than ever, we are on our own.

"And then Washington tries a big PR campaign to soothe us. Spontaneous, unrehearsed town meetings, planned down to the last straw bale for people to sit on. Up front, the suits to tell us their corporations are dandy-fine, peachy-keen, and everything will be just marvy after January first. Like any good corner therapist, they succeed in lulling us, because we want to be reassured, spared the unpleasant truth.

"We've always been very good at self-deception, at accepting what we want to hear . . . until the chips come clacking down. Then we pull together and do what has to be done.

"Somewhere a while back—after, say, nineteen seventy-six—our distrust of government turned to indifference. Our apathy rolled on through the eighties and into the nineties; it's visible in the voting percentages. Twenty-odd percent of those eligible actually elect our president. Who cares?

"Given this stinking situation, we know Washington barely affects our lives. The state capitol is closer, but it's just a building with a shiny dome and a couple of neighbors who owe their seats to interests we cannot relate to.

"So, long and short, we know we're on our own when it comes to Y2K, no matter what the smoothies tell us. We're disillusioned skeptics now, at the millennium.

"We could say government has let us down—again. But truth is, life has always been up to us, hasn't it? And y'know, maybe it sounds a little kooky, but I catch myself wondering if Y2K isn't an item we should listen to. Is there something going on here we're supposed to discover for ourselves?"

He let the monologue hang there for a minute, then the canyons of the Aronowitz grin deepened. "Some of us are making our own Y2K preparations quietly. Folks like you and me have overextended our credit cards; we've bought cases of Froot Loops and of macaroni-and-cheese. Some of us bought bulk supplies of wheat and rice, beans, dried fruits, MREs—that's the military acronym for Meals Ready to Eat, which we used to call rations—but then we forgot to store our supplies in ratproof containers. Or we didn't think to buy plastic buckets and store the grains under a nitrogen seal. And now, as we inspect our stockpiles, we see, to our horror, they've been breeding grubs and mites, or that some of the grain is sprouting."

Jim felt a connection, a lurch of affection for the old warrior who could so easily admit his humanity, his fallibility, to the public. It was what made him popular among people who had been there, done that. And the references to Washington reminded Jim that he himself hadn't done much after the initial stages of vice-presidential research he had committed to. Well, perhaps it wasn't surprising when you thought about it—since they hadn't called him back. He shook his head and tuned back in to *Compass*.

"So, whatever," Aronowitz was saying. "We bought five-gallon plastic bottles for water, filled them, then stacked them on floors that simply couldn't take the weight." Aronowitz smiled mischievously, the wry grin of a reporter who had seen too much grasping and power madness in one lifetime yet still tried to converse sensibly with viewers who vibrated to his wavelength. "After the commercials, we're going to talk with Carol Giroux and roll some tape to show you what we're talking about."

Compass's reporter had been out on the land to do a piece on the mood far from Manhattan's buzzing circuitry and Washington's self-aggrandizing halls. Not everything she found was pleasant.

"These are still the early days in a puzzling wave that is sweeping the country," Giroux noted. "Maybe it is a harbinger of . . . social experimentation," she said, a bit hesitantly. This was not a thought Americans were comfortable with. "We tend to stick to the basics. We don't like to be categorized. But you get whiffs of something going on . . . somewhere. And it's not an aberration."

Y2K, she had found, was an exemplary concentrator of minds among countless citizens. She picked her words with care. Carol knew she walked on ground that could shift at any moment as she tried to chart the fault line of what might be a major social upheaval, well before social seismologists started to catalog the rumbles and stress points.

Giroux stared unflinchingly into the camera lens. "Generations of my own people have had reason to distrust, even be disgusted by, the political establishment. We felt anger and contempt for the machinations that kept us in bondage. It's interesting to me, as an African American reporter doing a story among mostly white folks, that the distrust we have felt for generations is now endemic among Whitey. And just like Si, I feel unease. People are worried. Scared. But quietly, privately, in their family rooms.

"When they get scared, they blame Government, with a capital *G*, for not having leveled with them and for not taking care of them. We African Americans have felt the same way—for generations. But the real message is, we're all on our own. We've got to help each other. Simple. And that may be the social revolution. 'Big Daddy ain' goin' ta do it fo' us, no way!'

"Maybe we ought to call it devolution. Devolution of power from government, from institutions . . . back to the people, to what we call the grass roots. This power takes various forms and has numerous quiet leaders. Not the brash, out-front noisemakers, but the quiet ones you recognize because of the clearness in their eyes, the sureness with which they walk through difficult situations. The power is in the being and the doing, and that's where I think the message lies, just waiting to be discovered. But the only person who can find it is *you*. This assignment has made me more sure than ever that locally is where the action that counts lies.

"This is a major transition, folks. You can snipe at it. You can ride with it. Or you can get off at the next stop and watch it roll on by. But it seems to be happening now."

The camera backed off to include Si, sitting there spellbound by his reporter. The thought never would have occurred to him to impose his presence.

"There's something else too," Carol added, her hand sweeping out toward the plains and mountains, the cities and coasts. "We as a nation may be prepared to the nth for Y2K, but when the effects in Asia and South America and Europe come to be felt here, in this country . . . I leave that contemplation open.

"And so, back to you, Si, my friend. What do you make of all this?"

Jim had been following, but as if he were in a dream state. Now something stirred him. He watched as Si went into his closeout. "It makes me ask again: *Is Y2K a harbinger of something far more significant than a few computer glitches?* And—whatever may happen—will we as individuals, as Americans, summon our good common sense to deal with it?

"Carol Giroux and I leave you with that thought. Just this once, I'm going to close with a message from one of our most distinguished presidents, Franklin Delano Roosevelt, who said, 'The only thing we have to fear is fear itself.' Good night and good luck!"

Jim clicked off and sat in his chair for some time, wide awake, thinking.

Next morning, a bit later than usual, Jim sat in his office to put together what he knew or had heard. Back in the fall of 1998, when he had started to coalesce a good number of solid citizens, what he hoped to achieve wasn't clear, even to him. Awareness. Preparedness. Realism. The following winter, the group he had pulled together held standing-room-only meetings in the local high school gymnasium. But then the community's interest cooled, and the group withered. Maybe it was because of the call of the real world—jobs, families, stock market, America's military engagements abroad. Or because of the American attention span.

Jim persisted. He kept track of national Y2K news that had a local bearing and circulated it to those whose e-mail addresses he had, sometimes hesitant since he might be overburdening them; but he persevered, insistent that others be informed of the often alarming knowledge that was coming in on the Internet. Some of his own Y2K group tried to place orders for bulk foodstuffs from the supply houses that had sprung up on the Net. They were generally rebuffed with variations on a terse message: "Out of stock. Try again later."

Then Jim learned that small generators were becoming scarce, and that the Japanese were racing to ship in container loads, having cornered the products of Chinese manufacturers. Meanwhile, the 800 number at Schoenherr's Utility Hardware Emporium in southern Ohio, an Amish standby for generations, was perpetually busy. Schoenherr's specialized in old-fashioned nonelectric machinery, hand saws, scythes, equipment for horse-drawn wagons, manual water purifiers, and the like. The store also had disconnected its fax line.

In addition, companies that made heavy-duty water containers were running extra shifts. Businesses that manufactured freeze-dried foods for mountaineers and wilderness trekkers couldn't keep up with demand. Space blankets, which maintained body warmth, were in short supply. The food supplement and vitamin industries were swamped.

The Y2Kers were even more surprised when spam messages showed up in their e-mail in-boxes, indicating the supplies they had been interested in were now available from warehouses in Los Angeles—at prices at least double those quoted earlier by the Y2K houses.

Members of the dwindling Santa Ynez Valley committee turned to Jim with questions. "What's going on? No one's ever heard of these LA outfits. But now when I surf the Net, they're all over the place." Or "Some kind of scam going on? You heard from those Washington contacts of yours? Anything out of Sacramento?"

"Let me do some checking and I'll get back to you" was Jim's thoughtful reply.

When he got home, he dialed Sheriff Mike's direct line and relayed the stories he had heard at the meeting. "Don't suppose you could ask your fed friends if they know anything about this, could you? My people are pretty shook up. Of course, they should have placed their orders a lot sooner, but hell, we're all procrastinators, aren't we?"

A day later, Sheriff Mike called back. "On that matter you mentioned? Yeah, my contacts know all about it. It's the subject of a major investigation. They suspect a big-time scam, but that's all they could say. International ramifications. Slippery bunch. Pretty highly classified . . . Doesn't help you much, but that's all I can get."

Jim, caught off guard, paused and recalibrated. His primary goal had to remain, as always, to tell people that if they were prepared, if they kept calm, everything would turn out all right. With preparation, the ride through Y2K might be a bit rough, but everyone would bounce back.

CHAPTER TEN

Santa Ynez Valley
December 27, 1999

As soon as Jim entered the high school auditorium, he sensed that something wasn't quite right. He was thirty minutes early, and already there were double the number of people he'd seen at previous Y2K meetings. But then, this was the last one, at least for the year.

He'd tried to wriggle out of chairing the event since it was only two days after Christmas, but had been persuaded it was his civic duty by comments such as: "You started this, and you've been all around the country talking. How about bringing the home folks up to speed?"

It could have been an audience in any Western suburban community. Maybe there were a few more shiny new trucks in the parking lot, but not a lot of DKNY swank or The Gap's khaki chic. Perhaps even a bit of dressing down for the occasion—except for those who habitually bellied up with silver buckles the size of soup bowls, and the usual number of heavily painted ladies shoehorned tightly into elasticized riding britches that plunged into exotically tooled cowboy boots. There were sallow Hollywood transfers—in purple-dyed sackcloth jackets, raw silk shirts, and significant tennies—present to show solidarity with their brethren and sistern, the common folk. Then a scattering of Chumash, who had a vested interest in keeping their wildly profitable casino open. And a few watchful leathery Latinos who worked on Valley ranches, brought by their employers in a gesture of democracy, or perhaps as chauffeurs in case there was drinking after the meeting.

In addition to these regulars, Jim noticed dozens of newcomers in the unmistakable faded denim and with the plentiful long hair that marked those known as mountain people, or Teotwawkis. He was undecided whether their presence in such numbers was a good omen or not. It took a lot to get so many of them down from the Los Padres. But of course, it was the last meeting.

Up on the stage, Jim called for order promptly on the hour. To one side of the auditorium, a KSQK cameraman, porta-cam on his shoulder, and a second-string reporter were ready and waiting. Tonight's session was scheduled to include wrap-up reports on preparedness from the public utilities—water and power—and messages from FCNB&T president Bob Greensmith, as well as a spokesman for local food and hardware retailers.

The two utilities reps led off. They read formally, uncomfortably, from prepared statements jigsawed by PR flacks and then sanded by in-house legal departments. The placebos were nearly replicates of each other: "We are compliant. We have tested. We are prepared. We have, of course, practiced due diligence and have assurance from our vendors that their services to us are compliant with the high standards upon which we insist, and are in fact in order."

The water rep was smart enough to be brief and get out clean. He backed up his reassurances by pointing out that even in the most unlikely event of temporary shortages, water could be trucked in, even supplied by purification units at Lake Cachuma.

The crowd was not pleased with these formalized protestations, even though they were uttered by popular community figures. It took no genius to realize that if the power went down, everything would go to hell in a handbasket. Water pumps would not work without juice, communications would black out, and on and on.

Then two of the mountain women started to pillory the hapless representative from the electric company. Carlos Rodriguez, his corded neck straining at his top shirt-button, sweated but kept his cool. Jim noticed his fists clenching and unclenching behind his back.

As the women's contempt unrolled, it became apparent they had drawn their information, and their venom, from hard-core survivalist sources. "Mister Rodriguez," one said, "there's nothing personal in this, but how do you know that what your bosses are telling you is right? They've lied before!"

The second woman jumped in. "Mister Rodriguez, I might even believe what you're telling us except there's the Diablo Canyon nuke station just up the road. What if Diablo goes down?" There was a long pause, a hush, then, "Do we have meltdown? What exactly would happen?"

"Nothing," he replied finally. "There is absolutely no danger . . ." He stumbled on, into platitudes without facts, weathering the impatient buzz of the audience, for another few minutes before throwing his hands up and taking his seat.

Jim had to call for order, plead for courtesy. Here and there, people were leaving, but it was still SRO. Some of the folks, including the Teotwawkis, were using their cell phones. He had to tell himself that his instinct was wrong about the tension getting worse. And then, while he was introducing Bob Greensmith, he heard Mike's beeper go off and watched him step back in the stage wing to tend to *his* cell phone.

Greensmith took a number of hard hits when he did his "We'll have plenty of money if you'll please not try to get so much out all at the same time" thing, even rattling off numbers to show that cash demands and emptied savings accounts had far exceeded the usual Christmas "norms." People booed, hissed.

Greensmith sat down, red faced. Sheriff Mike came back to the table. Jim introduced the spokesman for local hardware and grocery stores. Things calmed down a little while the spokesman went on with his explanation that, with no room for stockpiling, no store could sustain abnormal demands if they exceeded the rate of delivery. "Please, folks," he pleaded, "if everyone can just, for example, buy less water, a little bit at a time, the supply—"

He was cut off by one of the Teotwawkis, a tall older man with a silver mane of hair, who abruptly stood and said, "We have heard all this more than once, sir. Our concern is about the supply of water, not to mention food, being cut off, controlled, and rationed."

Applause and whistles came up from all around. Jim noticed that the survivalists made up almost half the audience.

"Further," the silver-maned speaker continued, "it is obvious that we will come under, be *oppressed by*, martial law, since no other visible plan has been forthcoming from Washington." To this, a chorus of boos and applause rose up, along with shouting in less-than-polite language. More people stood to leave, muttering aloud, cursing. Near the entrance doors, a scuffle started up.

Jim got to his feet, raising both hands and calling for order.

"The Army will have to take over," the Teotwawki continued as the crowd backed off. "We have been lied to, are *being* lied to. We are in danger, all of us, and the government—"

"Sir!" Jim cut him off. "The government and the military, the Army as you put it, has nothing to do with this meeting. Our concern is for local—"

"Sir," the Teotwawki shot back, "it has *everything* to do with this meeting. And that is why we are here. When you see Army trucks rolling down the street, you'll know we were right."

Someone called out, "Sit down, you commie asshole!"

Now Jim sensed danger. The crowd, many of whom were on their feet, turned against one another. The locals wanted the mountain people shouted down—and out. Epithets crisscrossed over the audience. He scrambled for words.

"All of you here tonight," said the silver-hair in a ringing voice, raising his arms, "may not know that yesterday afternoon two hundred armed military troops set up a base camp over at Cachuma. We are watching them. We know, for instance, they spent most of today practicing formations, movements, carrying—besides their weapons—riot shields and truncheons. They were practice-firing tear gas. If we—"

Sheriff Mike stood so abruptly that the man stopped speaking. "Now sir," Mike said evenly, "how about we take this back where it belongs." Even the sheriff got boos and hisses, mostly from the mountain people. "Just cool down, everyone," Mike went on. "We are aware, you bet, that a National Guard unit is on a training exercise over at Lake Cachuma. Whenever they travel, they liaison with law enforcement. Nothing new. Now, you folks who live up in the forest—"

"Send the goddamn hippies home, Mike," someone yelled.

On one side of the auditorium another scuffle broke out. Carlos Rodriguez and Bob Greensmith got up and headed for the wings. Jim, still standing, moved closer to Mike.

"We'll send 'em home, Mike!" called a rancher.

It was hopeless, Jim knew. He stood mute.

"*All right, people,*" Mike suddenly bellowed. "This meeting is *over*. You will all exit *quietly* and *promptly*, and *any* disturbance that occurs will be dealt with *on* the spot. Now, good night!" Hands on his hips, he glared at the crowd.

As one, they stood and headed for the exits. Mesmerized, Jim watched.

"Let 'em blow it outside," Mike said without looking over. Again his beeper went off, and with one hand still on his hip he took out his radio phone and listened. Jamming it back in his belt case, he said to Jim. "Come on, pardner. You stick with me. "

Sweaty and shaken, Jim followed Sheriff Mike out to the parking lot. All the noise and hollering and cars, the cold blue lights keeping the dark away, reminded him of game time—until the ugly sounds of fist-fighting and the crash of a breaking bottle came to him. Like in a dream, a nightmare.

Mike opened the door to his Explorer and got on the RT. Meanwhile, Jim stared over the parked cars, listening to chaos. Red-and-blue lights from the vehicles of Mike's deputies flashed in two places. "This may turn bad," Mike was saying to his dispatcher in a flat voice. "Go to Condition Yellow. Call highway patrol. Buellton and Santa Maria, stand by to reinforce Santa Ynez substation as needed. See if Santa Barbara and Ventura can help us. Watch commander, get the next shift in now—get *everybody* in now. Better alert County Fire and the paramedics too. Call one ambulance down here right now.

"And open up the National Guard net. I want to be able to reach the commander of that exercise they're holding, in case we'll need 'em. Got it?"

Jim slumped against the car. All he could say was, "No Guard . . . no Guard."

"Come on, pardner. Climb aboard. Let's see how things are in the parking lot here." They cruised slowly down the rows of cars, many of which were pulling out. "Reason I'm having you tag along is that maybe you can calm a few down with your Y2K talk. My patience gets a little thin when folks start beating up on each other."

Jim was too stunned to reply. He couldn't understand why the meeting had flared up like it did. Mike's radio crackled with reports of disturbances and property damage, distress calls. People were being taken into custody. Curious citizens were jamming the phone lines.

Mike stopped where his deputies had cuffed two young men, both bleeding slightly from the mouth and nose, their clothing ripped. He motioned a deputy over.

"Throw 'em in the back," he said in a quiet voice. "Haul 'em around while you deal with the next problem, then let 'em go when you have to cuff another idiot. Same with the drunks. Take their keys, get their names and addresses, and send 'em home, OK? How does it look?"

"Can't figure it out," the deputy answered. "Too much going on."

"Stay cool," Mike said, easing ahead.

From the radio transmissions, Jim was able to piece together the unfolding events. A portion of the crowd had apparently formed a stream of rhythmically honking cars until a sheriff's unit with flashing blue-and-red lights stopped them cold near the old Mission Santa Ines. Others, grateful for the chance to escape a mounting confrontation, were peeling out of the parking lot and going home. Back in their family rooms, they'd switch on KSQK and wait. The local station had not yet responded to the flurry of traffic on its scanners. It was, after all, Monday night, and for the B team, the weather report and football scores were about as lively as it usually got.

Almost an hour had passed since the breakout at the high school. In the parking lot, the crowd was still surprisingly large—perhaps two hundred people. Some of those Mike and Jim passed were arguing vociferously, on the verge of fighting. Mike talked them down, politely ordered them home. Others were drinking; they got Mike's cold, silent stare before he moved on. One driver had collided with another who, unable to see because of an SUV parked next him, had backed out too soon. The two were in each other's faces, having left their crunched vehicles in place, which now blocked the aisle. Horns were blaring. Mike got out, spoke curtly to both, and ordered them back behind the wheel.

Another deputy came on Sheriff Mike's radio. "Sir, lots more people in the streets than usual, and they're heading toward town."

"Ten-four. Watch commander, check on the CHP and Santa Barbara backup. And Ventura. Should be just about at the pass now. Have the Santa Maria unit move down. Any calls from Sacramento, I'll handle them personally."

"Copy that." The watch commander was a seasoned sergeant due to be a lieutenant. "Anything else, Sheriff?"

"Yeah, get County Fire and the paramedics ready to move on short notice. Tell the fire chief I just might need to use his trucks as water cannon."

Once again Jim's instinct told him something was going wrong.

"Don't you start feeling guilty about any of this," Mike was saying. "Part of the problem is the holidays. Lots of people off work for the week, with time to screw around. And do a lot of drinking. Also, between Christmas and New Year's, people get bummed out, like all the magazine articles say. Incidents of suicide and family disturbances go way up . . . 'Tis the season to be jolly."

Jim knew Mike was listening with one ear to his radio, which was crackling constantly at low volume.

"Forgot about that," Jim said. "So you add the Y2K thing to the mix . . . people waiting till after Christmas to do something about it, or even think about it. It's the eleventh hour and everybody's getting uptight, which is what we're seeing now. I guess the timing of our meeting wasn't too—"

"Whoa." Mike raised his hand to cut him off, bent closer to the radio. Jim couldn't understand the dispatcher's words, other than "eleven-ninety-nine," whereupon Mike reacted instantly, flipping switches and accelerating. The siren startled Jim out of his wits. Red-and-blue lights flashed across the Explorer's white hood.

"Buckle up real tight," Mike ordered. "And hang on."

The next few minutes were more terrifying for Jim than anything he could remember. He clung to whatever he could grip as Mike rocketed through red lights, weaved in and out of traffic, spoke in codes to the dispatcher. Mike's swerving made him queasy. With the SUV's high center of gravity, every turn was a heart-stopper. He braced himself for a rollover.

When they roared up to Anderson's Maxi Market, Jim saw what looked like another small riot. Dozens of people were pushing loaded shopping carts through the crowd. Fights were in progress. Carts had tipped over, scattering boxes and cans that others were scooping up. Customers who had brazenly parked at the entrance were tossing groceries into open trunks.

Mike cut the siren as he stopped. Before he could get out, a young supermarket employee came up. "Sheriff, are we glad to see you. They're going crazy! We were trying to close, but the lines were so long people just started rolling their carts out the door without paying. Now *nobody*'s paying!"

Jim could see that Mike's arrival had done nothing to change the situation. Right in front of them the mayhem continued. He heard glass breaking, saw liquids of various hues pooling across the pavement. Two women were swinging wildly at each other, unaware their loaded carts were being snatched away.

Mike yanked out his bullhorn, called for order, threatened arrest. Nobody paid attention. He came back to his radio, turned up the volume, barked questions and orders.

Hypnotized by the chaos, Jim stared out windshield. Before him, in the glow of headlights, unfurled a scenario he had feared for years: the brute panic of order disintegrating, one neighbor pulling another's hair over half a case of baked beans. Would it snowball now, he wondered, triggered by the media?

"The back! Around the back!" another employee yelled through Mike's window. "They've got trucks!"

Mike waved him away as he busily responded to the incoming messages. "The Guard commander!" he was saying. "Now!" Then he turned the volume down and slumped in his seat.

"Sheriff . . . you can't call the Guard. That would really make a mess of things."

Mike took off his hat. "We've lost it, pardner. I've got zero backup. Nobody has backup." His voice was flat, resigned. "It gets better: someone, probably from out of town, had it figured out, organized. Trucks. Could be they stirred up some of the trouble to distract us, get us spread out too thin. They hit three other food stores at once . . . and both hardware supply . . . *This*," he said, gesturing with his chin at the crowd jamming the market's doorway, "is nothing. It's going to be a long night."

Major Dick McGuinn, a real estate specialist in one of Santa Barbara's prosperous multipartner law factories, was still in combat gear. He chewed a cigar as he answered Sheriff Mike's call, patched through from Sacramento National Guard headquarters. "Yeah, what's up? You're the last guy I expected to hear from out here. Wanna haul me in for indecent exposure?"

The sheriff was not amused. He briefed McGuinn succinctly. "This thing is out of control. I know it's irregular, but can you truck on into town, like at warp speed? Just your presence—say a dozen or so people—might calm things down."

"Sure would like to help you, Mike, but I'd have to get orders from the NG bureau at the governor's office." McGuinn was fully aware the conversation was being routinely recorded in Sacramento.

The sheriff was unswayed by bureaucratic niceties. "They can court-martial me, then. I'll take responsibility. My backups from Ventura and Santa Barbara can't get here fast enough. Major, it's a lot easier to put out a fire when it's just starting than when it's raging; I need a bigger hose. I'll see what I can do about Sacramento. And it might be easier to stay in touch by cell phone, if you have one. I'll give you my number . . ."

After they exchanged numbers, Major McGuinn somewhat nervously ordered his first sergeant to call the company into formation in the campground parking lot. He was unenthusiastic about going anywhere without clearance, but damned if this wasn't exactly the civil disorder they'd spent the day training for. It was the catch to command, pure and simple: you had to make decisions on the spot, with the best information available. Flexibility. Sure as hell, if he sat on his hands and the sheriff's rumble turned ugly, they'd land on him with both feet for not responding. Besides, his refusal to act without appropriate orders was already on tape in Sacramento.

See, he reminded himself, the sheriff was quick to decide. And sharp enough to suggest cell phones . . . which would bypass Sacramento. With any luck, it would be a false alarm and some damn good training.

Master Sergeant Leroy "Sour" Lemmon, a veteran of Desert Storm, was the usually raucous owner of a car repair business on a Santa Barbara side street. Now he hustled the troops into order with his usual professional finesse: "Shit's hit the fan, you clowns. C'mon, lard-asses—saddle up, get your riot gear, and fall in!"

When the company was assembled, McGuinn consulted with Lemmon and announced the plan. First platoon would stay to mind the store. They'd take second platoon—four squads—into town, put third and fourth platoons on stand-by. Better, he reasoned, to have twice as many as the sheriff requested so there'd be a reserve. The unit's six-by-six trucks growled to life, their vertical exhausts puffing in the thin night air.

Fifty-one men piled into three trucks and drove off behind McGuinn's Humvee with Sergeant Lemmon at the wheel. The ugly-snouted Army diesels roared down to State Highway 154.

"Sheriff, this is Shorty Henderson, Woodside Texaco, up two-forty-six near the forest."

"What can I do for you, Shorty?"

"Sheriff, we—Hildy and me—just saw something I think you oughta know about."

"Go on, Shorty."

"About two minutes ago, a whole damn convoy, maybe eight or ten open trucks came by here, headed south. They had camouflage paint and were full of men. I did see some weapons, I'm sure of it. And they weren't military."

"Eight to ten open trucks. Two minutes ago. You're absolutely sure you saw weapons?"

"Sure as shit, Sheriff."

"Shorty, just how far are you from one-fifty-four?"

"Seven-point-five miles, Sheriff."

"Gotta go, Shorty. Thanks a whole bunch. I owe you one."

"Major McGuinn, this is Mike Propoulos. Can you hear me?"

"Loud and clear, Sheriff. We're rolling. Can you hear me?"

"Real good. Major, we have big trouble. Tell me where you are, please."

"All I know is we're coming up one-fifty-four, looking for two-forty-six. We got the pedal to the metal. What's up?"

"Listen close, Major. *Keep* the pedal there. How long you been on the road?"

"Five minutes, maybe more."

"Good. Listen, you'll probably reach two-forty-six in about ten more minutes. At the intersection, split your group however you choose. Send about half over here. That's a left turn—repeat, left turn—onto two-forty-six, clear? The trouble is coming down two-forty-six from the right—repeat, right—and should arrive about the time you get there. Follow me?"

"Affirmative, Sheriff. What exactly is this 'trouble'?"

"Eight or ten light trucks, painted camouflage, carrying armed men—repeat, armed. I know it sounds crazy, but a friend of mine called in to report it and I believe him."

"What the hell kind of—?"

"Just listen, Major. My guess is that it's a militia group from up in the Los Padres boondocks—survivalists, Armageddon types. My next guess is that some of their people raising hell over here in the street managed to call them down. And my third guess is that they'll be on top of you at that intersection in the next ten minutes. You must—"

"Hold it, Sheriff—Sergeant, faster, *faster!* Pour it on!—OK, Sheriff, go ahead."

"Major, you must intercept these individuals, stop them at any cost. And Jesus, not in the middle of one-fifty-four. Turn right on two-forty-six and set up a roadblock, anything, away from the highway. Can you do that?"

"*Jay*-sus, Mary, and Joseph, Mike."

"Major, if you miss them and they get into town, we'll have a situation I don't even want to think about. If they don't show up in ten minutes, beat it on over here. Can you handle this?"

"Do my best, Sheriff. I'll get back to you when roadblock is secured. Over and out."

"What was all that about, sir?" Sergeant Lemmon asked over the wind and engine noise.

"You won't believe it, Sergeant. I'll explain in a minute. Faster, faster. Watch for the two-forty-six sign. At the intersection, we pull over. Got it?"

"Affirmative, sir."

"I'm sending Lieutenant Burke on into town with two trucks. We have something else to do." McGuinn was sweating, and his heart was racing under his field jacket. How the *hell* could this happen? he wondered. What if—

"Two-forty-six sign ahead, sir. One mile."

"Don't slow down till we get there, Sergeant. When we pull over, keep the engine running, lights flashing."

McGuinn prayed for light traffic, aware that thus far vehicles had been passing them like bats out of hell. Jesus, if only they could be sure there were no black-and-whites around . . .

Sergeant Lemmon flicked the right turn signals. McGuinn unstrapped his seat belt. When the Humvee rolled to a stop on the gravel shoulder, he leaped out to talk to the drivers of the three trucks behind them.

Coming back, he was breathing hard. "Turn right here, Sergeant. Good. Keep the speed up. We have to set up a goddamn roadblock." In the beam from their lights, McGuinn saw only an empty two-lane road ahead. On both sides was grassland, a few trees. He searched for oncoming headlights. Nothing.

"OK, here."

The Humvee, followed by the remaining six-by-six, crunched to a stop on the shoulder. Within five minutes, the squad of twelve men was offloaded, briefed, told to lock and load their M-16s, and dispersed in the grass along the road—six on each side, several yards apart. The squad leader had an RT-pack so he could stay in contact with Sergeant Lemmon.

McGuinn positioned the six-by-six diagonally across the pavement, with headlights and yellow flashers on. The driver was ordered to prepare to set flares. The Humvee straddled the yellow line, also with flashers and headlights on. Both engines were turned off.

In the Humvee's headlights, McGuinn dialed Mike. "This is McGuinn, Sheriff. Roadblock in place. Over and out."

Accompanying Mike's quick "Thank you, sir" was the sound of sirens in the background.

Lemmon lifted the feed-tray cover of the M-60 machine gun on the Humvee's mounting post, set up the ammunition feed, and charged the gun. The metallic *clack* of the pulled bolt seemed extra loud, and serious.

Now it was quiet. Neither man had opted to don his helmet—at Lemmon's suggestion. McGuinn pulled his cap a little more snugly over his forehead and looked at his watch. He could almost hear his heart working. He didn't let himself worry about arriving too late; part of him hoped they had. They'd wait for ten, maybe fifteen, minutes like Mike had said, then mount up and head for town. In the silence, he could hear the Humvee's engine ticking as it started to cool.

"Sergeant?" he said finally.

"Yessir."

"Would you agree that a bunch of trucks carrying armed men falls under the category of civil disorder?"

"Yessir. Absolutely."

"Therefore, are we not also preparing to neutralize hostile elements?"

"Yessir. I'd say we are."

"Good. Just checking, Sergeant."

Oh balls, McGuinn thought. *How did this happen? Never heard a shot fired in anger in my life and here comes a* horde *of armed lunatics*—American *armed lunatics. How* many *armed lunatics, and armed with what?* Jay-*sus, Mary, and Joseph.* "Sergeant?"

"Yessir."

"You ever been in a firefight . . . over in the Gulf?"

"Yessir. Mixed it up with the towel-heads couple dozen times."

"Think this will get hot? Jesus, Sour, we *can't* get into a goddamn shooting match here . . . I'll be on the bullhorn. What's your advice?"

"First, we show force; we've got that. Next, talk 'em down. Tell them to go home ASAP—or they go to prison. Tell 'em if they fire a single shot they're dog meat."

"Dog meat . . ." McGuinn rubbed his forehead. "And if they fire on us?"

"Stay low. Stay cool. Like we told the squads. Return fire only when fired upon. Aim to maim, not to kill. Don't sweat it, Major. These guys gotta be pussies. You'll see."

McGuinn's three squads in two six-by-sixes, under the command of twenty-two-year-old Second Lieutenant B. Bob Burke, were met by one of Mike's deputies who'd been dispatched for escort. They were led to the shopping center where the looting of Anderson's Maxi Market was still going strong. The KSQK news truck had arrived; the mastcam was up, and the crew was scrambling to get the big lights operational. The escorting deputy answered Mike's call and found him behind the market, at the loading docks, where he had single-handedly arrested four men at gunpoint. All were from Los Angeles. Two carried handguns. Both trucks had false plates. With Jim watching, crouched in the Explorer under stern orders from Mike, the sheriff had caught them loading their trucks. Having only two sets of handcuffs, he had cuffed the men in pairs, one to the other. They were lying face-down on the pavement when the deputy arrived.

Lieutenant Burke's thirty-six men dismounted, donned riot gear, and fell into riot control formation at the far end of the parking lot. They drew a hundred enthusiastic spectators, many of whom were suddenly ex-looters. When the formation of weirdly attired, gas-masked soldiers was complete, the crowd broke into applause.

Sheriff Mike, with Jim still at his side, got on the bullhorn and warned everyone in the store that they were about to be tear-gassed and taken into custody. While the former was imminently likely, the latter was far beyond Mike's, or the troops', capability—although none of the looters figured this out.

By the time the National Guard formation reached the front of the market, there wasn't a single looter inside.

* * *

Fred Georgeson peered nervously ahead, hands tight on the steering wheel, watching the blacktop in his headlights and cursing his own stupidity and temerity. Beside him, Dean smoked. The wind in the cab made Dean's cigarette glow orange in the dim light from the dash.

Fred, to start with, was less than thrilled about being called up to drive after dark, and when he saw a dozen men piling in the back, wearing various camouflage apparel and carrying assault rifles and AK-47s, he knew he was in a place he didn't want to be. Not at all. Then, when they'd hooked up with six more trucks also loaded with armed men wearing various camouflage apparel, he freaked.

He was also nervous about Dean, who seemed somehow different. Fred's questions were discouraged. They were going down to town to "present a protective element of force," or some such horseshit, upon the occasion of the National Guard "threatening to confiscate and control water and food."

Dean, too, had a weapon of some sort; it was resting upright against the dash, held between his knees. Fred did not like weapons, especially now, since any contact with the law, and certainly the National Guard, could be very dangerous indeed.

Dean was urging him to go faster. Just past the Texaco station one of the trucks had had a flat, and Dean, who was clearly in charge of the expedition, had hustled men from the disabled truck into the remaining six, five of which were now following behind them.

"Just be cool, man," Dean said calmly for the hundredth time. "We're only going to show up so they pay attention to us. We're making a *statement*, man." He patted his weapon. "This isn't even loaded, Fred. Nobody's is loaded. Don't worry."

Fred *was* worrying, big time. He was dry-mouthed and trembly. In his rearview mirrors, the five trucks looked like fifty. This was major bad karma, no question.

Then ahead, he saw what looked like an accident. Two vehicles, with headlights on, were in the middle of the road—one cocked sideways, the other facing forward. Soon one, two, three red flares fizzed up bright on the pavement. He geared down, daring to be relieved that the accident would prevent them from going any further.

"What the—?" Dean said. "Oh, Christ . . . Turn on the emergency flashers."

Fred fumbled for the flasher switch, but when he saw that the vehicles were Army, he hit the brakes. And partially lost control of his bladder.

"God*dammit*," Dean whispered. "Easy now . . ."

Fred did what he could to bring the heavy truck to a safe stop, terrified of being rear-ended by the others. His right leg was spasming as he pushed down on the brake pedal. No more than thirty feet away was a sideways Army truck. In the middle of the road was one of those Humdingers, or whatever the fuck they were called, with a machine gun on a post. He could see only two soldiers, wearing caps. One stood by the Humdinger and the other in front of it, left hand on his hip and the right holding a bullhorn. Which he raised to his mouth.

"*Turn off your engine*," came the voice from the bullhorn.

"Turn it off!" Dean hissed, then reached over and spun the keys when he sensed Fred going catatonic. Fred, hands frozen on the wheel, looked around for more soldiers in the dark.

"*Dismount from the vehicle*," came the order. "*Both of you. Now!*"

"God*dammit*," Dean whispered again, opening his door and letting his weapon slide to the floor. "Come on, Fred. Move it. There's only two of them."

They both got out. The officer lowered the bullhorn and walked toward them, beckoning them both to come closer. Dean raised his hands a little and Fred did the same. Now they were side by side. Fred was shaking at the knees, and the cool night air made his wet pants cold.

"What's up?" the officer asked. Hearing no reply, he introduced himself. "I'm Major McGuinn, California National Guard. Either of you carrying weapons?"

Dean answered, "No, sir." Fred, too nervous to speak, shook his head no.

"I've been authorized," the major went on, "by the sheriff's department to detain you and your . . . group because we have a report that you might be armed. Is that true?" The major rested his hand on his holster.

When neither of them answered, the major asked Fred, "What's your name?"

"Fred."

The major turned to Dean. "And yours?"

"Dean, sir."

"Fred and Dean," said the major. "Well . . . Dean, you go down that line of trucks and tell them to turn their engines off, and their lights, OK? And then tell every swingin' dick in those trucks that *nobody* gets out of 'em, OK? And that if we so much as *see* a single weapon of any kind, things are going to go *all* to hell here. Got it?"

"Yessir." Dean backed up, walked off.

"Fred," the major said. "You get back in the truck and turn off the lights and sit real still, OK?"

Trembling, Fred did as he was told. After switching off the lights, he sat back in the seat, gripping the wheel, sweating like crazy. Everything was going to be OK, he told himself; he hadn't done anything really wrong. In the rearview mirrors he could see the lights of the other trucks going off. Then he heard engines rev up, and headlights filled *both* his mirrors as two trucks pulled up tight against his, one on each side, and stopped.

Oh God, he thought. In the glare of the headlights he saw the major back up to the Humdinger. Then he heard a *pop-pop-pop* from behind. *Oh God, the crazy bastards.* He saw the other soldier at the machine gun, which suddenly flashed yellow out of the muzzle as streaks of orange fire zipped toward the truck to his left, ripping into the engine and spraying sparks and pieces of glass over his own hood and through his open window, some striking his face. *Going to die,* Fred thought. He hit the passenger seat. And lost complete control of his bladder, hunching down as the fire-streaks raked his truck—*Oh God, help!*—banging and cracking and sparking, then moving on to his right. Fred twitched at the racket of bullets tearing at the other truck's engine, sending more sparks and glass into his cab.

And then silence.

Oh God, I'm alive. He was astonished. He heard noises . . . someone whimpering in the back of the truck . . . someone else calling out in fear . . . the hissing of steam from riddled radiators. He felt the truck list, realized the tires were deflating. He sat up, brushing glass and plastic fragments from his jacket. He turned to his left, saw the two men in the other truck sitting upright, one shaking his head. To his right both men were also upright, one still covering his face. None of the windshields were cracked. Pink smoke, tinted by the light of the flares, drifted by.

"*Now then, gentlemen,*" the major boomed through the bullhorn. "*Everyone will dismount . . .*"

To Fred, the major's voice was so strong and loud that it seemed to be coming from above, from a fatherly being. He was shaking so hard he could barely open the door and step down. Steamy puddles of coolant spread around his feet. Chips of glass and plastic glinted in the Humdinger's headlights. Soldiers, wearing helmets and carrying rifles, came out of the dark as the men crawled silently down from the trucks.

"*Dismount from the trucks,*" came the major's voice again. "*Dismount . . . and start walking . . . Dismount and start walking. Go home.*"

Two hours and fifty-five minutes after the National Guard arrived, order was restored.

Jim, exhausted, was still with Sheriff Mike. The backup units from Santa Maria to Ventura had set up checkpoints circling town and, along with CHP and Mike's deputies, had arrested twenty-six looters—including three more Los Angelenos and men from two more loaded trucks. In town, sixty-seven looters had been apprehended, along with a dozen drunks and troublemakers. There were no fatalities and no serious injuries. Property damage and loss, mostly to looted stores, was considerable.

Since all area jail cells were now occupied, those arrested were detained at the high school gym, where Sheriff Mike had enough room to process them. The high school, where it all started, became the center of the evening's events.

By the time Major McGuinn and Sergeant Sour Lemmon showed up, their little convoy—the Humvee and single six-by-six—had grown; three open, camouflage-painted trucks loaded with assault weapons brought up the rear. To clear the road, the other three trucks, leaking fuel and coolant from their thoroughly trashed engines, had been pushed into the ditch, where tow trucks would salvage them at first light.

McGuinn rode Patton-like into town, standing in the Humvee with a cigar in his teeth, waving. He was greeted along the streets with cheers and applause, and warmly welcomed by more cheers and applause at the high school—when he finally got around to finding it.

Sergeant Lemmon convened all personnel; had them park the vehicles in a perfect, close line in the lot; and called formation. McGuinn quickly went down the ranks—mindful of the TV cameras— and congratulated each man. This, too, drew an audience, many of whom were young women. Applause were generous.

When the parking lot filled up again, it became obvious to Sheriff Mike that the crowd was wanting something more, for once again they were in a festive mood. Faced with the nightmarish prospect of yet another disturbance, and pressured by the KSQK staff for some sort of "closure," Sheriff Mike rose to the occasion and told Jim to make a speech.

Mike tipped off the TV crew and assembled Jim and Major McGuinn at his side on the front steps of the high school. The TV lights pulled the crowd together. TV mike in hand, the sheriff led off with, "Many of you folks didn't behave too well this evening"—applause, whistling, and laughter—"and we still have plenty of room in the gym if you don't behave yourselves for the rest of the evening . . ." More applause and laughter. "This gentleman right here"—he motioned Major McGuinn closer—"came with his men to save our bacon, and he deserves our recognition." Applause. "And gratitude. Major McGuinn, California National Guard, Santa Barbara, would you say a couple of words?"

With the microphone in his face, McGuinn hesitated, then announced, "Mission accomplished."

To cheers and whistles, McGuinn stepped back, leaving Mike to introduce Jim as "one of our own, the Y2K man, as everybody knows."

Jim took a deep breath and tried to show a level of confidence he did not feel. Self-conscious of his bedraggled appearance, weary to the bone, and emotionally drained, he had no idea what he was going to say. All he knew was that his comments—like those uttered in the wake of the Steinhart tragedy and the bank run—were likely to be on network TV within twenty-four hours. The beauty, the perfection, the synchronicity of the opportunity struck him so forcefully that he shivered.

"C'mon, Jim!" came a shout form the crowd.

"C'mon, Dad," came another, from the second row.

"Thank you," he said finally, "but I don't deserve recognition tonight. If anything, I should take some blame. Sheriff Mike, Major McGuinn, and their people are the ones who deserve our thanks, and our gratitude.

"My special interest—some would say expertise—has been, and still is, Y2K and its problems and ramifications. What happened here earlier tonight was . . . a shock, a wake-up call, and a lesson. For us, and also for America. Thank God no one was seriously hurt. If you remember the Steinhart family, another lesson, you realize that as fallible humans we sometimes react to irrational fears in irrational ways, especially when we don't have all the information. The consequences can be tragic, as they were with the Steinharts; or disturbing, as in the bank run; or dangerous, like tonight was. As you can see, we sometimes cause our own troubles—turn against our neighbors, against each other. We can't do that, folks.

"What about Y2K, you ask? It's a computer problem, you know

that. Most of the computer problems have been fixed or will be fixed. It does no good to blame anyone, including the people in Washington, for repairs that have not yet been made. The problems we need to address are not those of machines, but those of human beings—you, me, everybody.

"Whatever Y2K problems surface in the coming weeks will happen right here in our hometown, and in every other hometown. To meet them, we must simply prepare for the worst, and I can tell you that the *very* worst will be temporary inconveniences, brief disruptions in utilities, and occasional shortages. All we need are enough basic necessities to last for a week or so. But we also need to keep our heads screwed on straight, maintain our cool. Someone—your child, your friend, your parent—could have gotten killed here tonight. We are all fortunate that no one did.

"Yes, this is the eleventh hour . . . four days to go. A lot of people have waited until the last minute to stock up, and earlier tonight some of them panicked, tried to get everything they could, and let fear take control. Folks, there is nothing to fear. Plenty of whatever we need is out there. We aren't going to run out of anything. Don't let fear . . . make you afraid.

"Next Saturday does not mark the end of the computer problem. Inconveniences and shortages may continue to turn up every now and then for months, until we get the details fixed. We can handle it. And how we behave will make all the difference. As Americans, we have always joined together to solve problems with common sense and courage.

"In the end, maybe Y2K will remind us to stick together, help one another. It may even make us stronger, and wiser. God bless and go home . . . Happy New Year."

CHAPTER ELEVEN

Santa Ynez Valley
December 28, 1999

The light bar on the approaching Explorer told Jim it was Sheriff Mike. A tunneling billow of grit followed, then overtook the vehicle, blew across the porch, and passed on. Mike pulled to an easy stop, then got out. His uniform, Jim noticed, was spiffy, starched and creased, and he wasn't wearing his hat or handgun.

"Evenin', Jim," Mike said.

"Sheriff. Looks like you've recovered from last night."

"Yeah. Hell on wheels, wasn't it? Turned out, while all that was going on, somebody hijacked a gasoline rig north of Santa Maria. Found it this morning, half empty. More of the same, huh?"

"Hmm. Probably. Ready for a cold one?"

"I'm ready for a case of cold ones, pardner. It so happens I laid myself off early. Thought I'd get a good start on the rest of the evening. Thought I'd begin here, if you're in the mood and got the time."

"You've earned it, Sheriff. And I'm in the mood and got the time."

They started in on the chilled green bottles. Mike meant business, Jim could see; over small talk, he put down three before Jim had two. He'd catch up, though. Seemed like a good idea. Kate was off at a party, and he sensed that Mike was bringing more than a thirst to this little visit. *Hombre a hombre.*

"After that Chinese fire drill last night," Mike began, "I got to thinking about this goddamn Y2K thing. And I'm looking for some straight, no-bullshit answers."

"Do my best, Sheriff."

"One day everything's quiet, and the next day we got normal folks blowing themselves up and tearing the bank apart, right? Next thing, we got a gang of pistol-packin' creeps from LA hijacking canned hams out of Anderson's, while more normal folks steal it bare. Not to mention a platoon of loonies heading into town with enough firepower to start World War Three . . . You should see *that* gun collection. All mine now; we've got the biggest nonmilitary arsenal in the whole state. So, my first question is, are we in for more of this? Hell, Jim, you know how close we came last night to putting the coroner to work?"

"I do, Mike. I can't believe it myself."

"Will there be more, is what I'm asking. Do I issue those AK-47s to my deputies for the weekend, call the Guard back, or what?"

"Will there be more?" Jim hesitated. "You saw what happened. People got scared, got stupid, and they—"

"Jim, people get *real* stupid. Then they get *dead*. My job is to keep that from happening. Yours, as I see it, has been pretty much the same—but you're the expert, pardner. Just what, exactly, is going to happen? Best guess, no bullshit. If you know more than you're telling me, I'd be real appreciative to—"

"Mike, there probably *will* be more, but it will all be local. Nothing catastrophic. No big collapse of, say, the electric company. Just stupid incidents. And not many, if we're lucky."

"That's not a lot of help, pardner. Maybe the Los Padres Ewok Liberation Army will attack at dawn, or maybe they won't. How did this . . . happen? I mean, besides all the computer stuff I don't want to hear about. Why didn't anybody upstairs tell us, warn us?"

"You mean Washington?"

"I mean Washington: the president, the vice president, the FBI, whatever. Christ, I sound like one of those Teo-whackos. You were in Washington—what is this, top secret?"

"Yeah I was, and no it isn't. There isn't any secret, Mike. It was all I could do to get them to sit still for one minute to listen. The president . . . well, he got a little busy, didn't he? Had a lot on his plate. Plus, he's a lame duck. Y2K didn't make his fix list. And the veep just blew it off, even though he's a techie. He could have shown some leadership. Y2K could have made a great campaign point. The truth is, Y2K aside, I don't think he's got the *cojones* anyway.

"The gamble in Washington, as I see it, Mike, is that Y2K will be no big deal—which I think, hope, is true. If it *is* a big deal, if it comes down, then they lost the gamble—and we eat it. Oops, just another all-so-typical screwup, lack of foresight."

Mike scratched his nose in thought, looking suspicious, before saying, "You, Jim—are you worried?"

"Nah . . . All there is to worry about is stupid people doing stupid things, like I said. Honest to God, Mike, that's about it."

"No bullshit, Jim?"

"No bullshit. Listen, neither Washington nor the big companies would tell us straight. Scared of liabilities and of public reaction. When they finally understood that fixes had to be made, they got a late start. They blew millions, billions, on last-minute fixes, still are, and only got half done, if you want to know the truth. So they're crossing their fingers, hoping everything will hold together and nothing too serious will happen."

"Your best guess?"

"My best guess is they're right. What I tried to do was . . . Well, what's the point now?"

Mike studied Jim, then turned back to his beer. "Liked your speech last night, by the way."

Jim shrugged. "God knows, I've made plenty of them."

"How come you got so riled when the KSQK people showed up at Anderson's? I thought you were going to kick Gerri LaPorte's butt."

"At first, I got riled—no, panicked—because the goddamn media has turned into a pack of bloodthirsty jackals. They show the worst; they overinflate and exaggerate danger, which causes everybody to overreact. They *create* trouble. All for ratings. Nobody with brains has any control. It's all tabloid theater. However, to be fair . . . Ah, forget it."

Sheriff Mike was studying the label on his bottle. "This," he sighed, "is what I needed. Loosen up. You gonna party New Year's Eve?"

"Haven't thought that far ahead, to tell the truth."

"Patty's putting something together. She wanted to ask you if she should prepare for a party or a disaster."

Jim found this funny enough to laugh at. Or maybe it was the brew. "Party," he chuckled.

"You're invited. Kate, too, if she hasn't got plans and if she's old enough to see adults crash and burn." Mike finished off his bottle. "Anything else we ought to do between now and then?"

"Nothin' I can think of. Except prepare to party."

The two men went quiet, looked out over the pale orange sunset and the mountains turning purple. Mike set his empty in the six-pack carton with the others.

"Time to go, pardner. Thanks for the refreshments." He held out his hand.

"You did good last night, Sheriff." Their handshake took a bit longer than usual. "You oughta get a damn medal."

Sheriff Mike ambled over to the Explorer and climbed in. Before closing the door, he said, "Jim . . . Best guess. What will happen the next morning, the first day?"

"Not much, pardner." Jim swirled the last of his beer around the bottom of his bottle, thinking, hoping it was the right answer. "But the news on TV might be pretty entertaining . . . You got a week's worth of stuff stashed away?"

"Patty-cakes, I do believe, has stored up enough toilet paper for the whole county." Mike slammed his door. "And I've got liquid reserves."

"That's all you need."

Jim held on to the railing upright, watching Mike's dust recede. In the silence, he was glad to be alone. Turning, he noticed the light shift while the sun slipped away, sending thin spears of gold over the valley. Everything seemed more sharply defined—more intensely cast in emeralds, violets, and saffrons—as darkness crept up from the canyons, crossed the grasslands, and shaded the mountains.

He felt relief and a deep serenity, as if a long journey had ended, bringing him home at last to Manzanita Ranch. He could sense Beth's presence all around him. *Beth,* he thought, his eyes burning, *I did the best I could. Thanks for your understanding.*

Her response was immediate. *"You've worked hard, Jim. You can be proud. Everyone's getting the message that Y2K is about people, not computers. But you're not done yet, darling. Y2K is no isolated incident; it's a harbinger of events to come. There's still more work ahead."*

APPENDIX

Primary Y2K Information Resources

Senate Special Committee on the Year 2000 Technology Problem
http://y2k.senate.gov
The committee, created on April 2, 1998, by unanimous consent of the Senate, is among the most broadly based and best informed Y2K bodies in existence.

President's Council on the Year 2000 Conversion
http://www.y2k.gov
Offers information on the federal government's efforts to prepare its computer systems, links to compliance data for critical sectors of the economy, and other resources.

Dr. Ed Yardeni's Economic Network
http://www.yardeni.com/cyber/html
The chief global economist at Deutsche Bank looks at Y2K's impact from a global economic perspective.

Y2K Update Report
http://www.y2kupdatereport.com
Y2K experts from around the world offer news and commentary.

The DavisLogic Y2K Information Center
http://www.DavisLogic.com
Steve Davis, a leading authority on Y2K risk management and community preparedness, provides information and commentary on numerous Y2K issues, with a focus on managing the associated risks.

Year 2000 Information Center
http://www.year2000.com/cgi-bin/y2k/NFyear2000.cgi
Peter de Jager, a leading authority considered by many to be a worldwide leader in creating awareness of the Y2K problem, presents relevant information.

Center for Strategic and International Studies (CSIS)
http://www.csis.org/html/y2k.html
CSIS's Y2K task force, composed of senior governmental officials and business leaders from the United States and abroad, assesses Y2K risks to the government, business community, consumers, financial markets, and global trading system.

Global 2000 Coordinating Committee
http://www.global2k.com
The committee, made up of more than 680 contacts in the financial services private sector from over 280 institutions and associations, representing more than 50 countries, identifies areas in which coordinated initiatives will improve the capacity of financial institutions worldwide to meet the year 2000 date change.

Year 2000 Canadian Federal Government
http://www.info2000.gc.ca
Contains information on the Canadian government's effort to prepare for and manage Y2K.

United Nations
http://www.un.org/members/yr2000
Included are links to the full text of "The Year 2000 Challenge for the United Nations" and four UN resolutions on the subject.

Emergency Management Information Resources

Internet Sites

American Red Cross Y2K Information
http://www.redcross.org/disaster/safety/y2k.html
Offers basic information on Y2K and related management tips for the general public.

Coalition 2000
http://www.coalition2000.org
Provides community preparedness guidelines, together with an excellent toolbox of resources.

Federal Emergency Management Agency (FEMA) Y2K Information
http://www.fema.gov/y2k/
Presents basic information on Y2K and related management tips for the general public.

International Association of Emergency Managers (IAEM)
http://www.iaem.com
IAEM is a nonprofit educational organization dedicated to promoting the goals of saving lives and protecting property during emergencies and disasters.

National Emergency Management Agency (NEMA)
http://nemaweb.media3.net/index.cfm
NEMA—the professional association of state, Pacific, and Caribbean insular emergency management directors—provides vital information and resources for state and territorial directors and governors.

Family and Community Contacts

For help on Y2K problems, first check with your local town hall. If you live in an unincorporated area, contact your County Hall of Administration.

Emergency services are often housed in the office of the chief executive of the local government body or in the fire, police, or public safety department.

The local office of the American Red Cross can provide you with a wealth of "all risk" management information, as well as direct you to the official Emergency Services office.

One of the above resources may also be able to guide you to a local volunteer civic-action Y2K group.

Emergency Services Offices

The following state-by-state listing of Emergency Management Offices has been compiled by the National Emergency Management Association.

Alabama
Lee Helms, Director
Office of the Governor
e-mail: leeh@aema.state.al.us

Alaska
Dave Liebersbach, Director
Military Department
e-mail: dave_liebersbach@ak-prepared.com

Arizona
Michael Austin, Director
Military Department
e-mail: austinm@dem.state.az.us

Arkansas
Director
Governor's Office
e-mail: w.harper@adem.state.ar.us

California
Dallas Jones, Director
Office of the Governor
e-mail: dallas_jones@oes.ca.gov

Colorado
Tom Grier, Director
Department of Local Affairs
e-mail: tom.grier@state.co.us

Connecticut
Daniel McGuire, Director
Department of Public Safety
e-mail: dmcguire.ctoem@juno.com

Delaware
Sean Mulhern, Director
Department of Public Safety
e-mail: jmulhern@state.de.us

Florida
Joseph Myers, Director
Department of Community Affairs
e-mail: joe.myers@dca.state.fl.us

Georgia
Gary McConnell, Director
Office of the Governor
e-mail: vbartlett@gema.state.ga.us

Hawaii
Roy C. Price Sr., Vice Director
Military Department
e-mail: rprice@scd.state.hi.us

Idaho
John Cline, Director
Military Department
e-mail: jcline@bds.state.id.us

Illinois
Mike Chamness, Director
Office of the Governor
e-mail: mchamness@pop.state.il.us

Indiana
Patrick Ralston, Director
Department of Public Safety
e-mail: pralston@sema.state.in.us

Iowa
Ellen Gordon, Administrator
Military Department
e-mail: ellen.gordon@emd.state.ia.us

Kansas
Gene Krase, Deputy Director
Military Department
e-mail: lekrase@agtop.state.ks.us

Kentucky
Ronn Padgett, Executive Director
Military Department
e-mail: rpadgett@kydes.dma.state.ky.us

Louisiana
Col. Michael Brown, Assistant Director
Military Department
e-mail: xbrown@hotmail.com

Maine
Bill Libby, Director
Military Department
e-mail: john.w.libby@state.me.us

Maryland
David McMillion, Director
Military Department
e-mail: dmcmillion@mema.state.md.us

Massachusetts
Bud Iannazzo, Acting Executive Director
Department of Public Safety
e-mail: bud.iannazzo@state.ma.us

Michigan
Insp. Ed Buikema, Deputy State Director
Department of Public Safety
e-mail: buikemae@state.mi.us

Minnesota
Kevin Leuer, Director
Department of Public Safety
e-mail: kevin.leuer@state.mn.us

Mississippi
James Maher, Director
Office of the Governor
e-mail: maher@memaorg.com

Missouri
Jerry Uhlmann, Director
Military Department
e-mail: juhlmann@mail.state.mo.us

Montana
Jim Greene, Administrator
Military Department
e-mail: jigreene@state.mt.us

Nebraska
Francis Laden, Director
Military Department
e-mail: fran.laden@nema.state.ne.us

Nevada
Frank Siracusa, Director
Department of Public Safety
e-mail: fss@quik.com

New Hampshire
Woodbury Fogg, Director
Office of the Governor
e-mail: wfogg@nhoem.state.nh.us

New Jersey
Kevin Hayden, Deputy Director
Department of Public Safety
e-mail: p000haydenk@smtp.lps.state.nj.us

New Mexico
Ernesto Rodriguez, Director
Department of Public Safety
e-mail: erodriguez@dps.state.nm.us

New York
Ed Jacoby Jr., Director
Military Department
e-mail: edward.jacoby@semo.state.ny.us

North Carolina
Eric Tolbert, Director
Department of Public Safety
e-mail: etolbert@dem.dcc.state.nc.us

North Dakota
Douglas Friez, Director
Military Department
e-mail: dfriez@state.nd.us

Ohio
Jim Williams, Acting Deputy Director
Department of Public Safety
e-mail: jwilliams@dps.state.oh.us

Oklahoma
Albert Ashwood, Director
Office of the Governor
e-mail: albert.ashwood@oklaosf.state.ok.us

Oregon
Myra Thompson Lee, Director
Department of State Police
e-mail: mlee@oem.state.or.us

Pennsylvania
Robert Churchman, Acting Director
Office of the Governor
e-mail: bchurchman@pema.state.pa.us

Rhode Island
Ray La Belle, Director
Military Department
e-mail: labelleR@ri-arng.ngb.army

South Carolina
Stan McKinney, Director
Military Department
e-mail: smmckinn@strider.epd.state.sc.us

South Dakota
John Berheim, Acting Director
Military Department
e-mail: john.berheim@dem.state.sd.us

Tennessee
John White, Director
Military Department
e-mail: jwhite@tnema.org

Texas
Tom Millwee, Director
Department of Public Safety
e-mail: tom.millwee@txdps.state.tx.us

Utah
Earl Morris, Director
Department of Public Safety
e-mail: pscem.emorris@state.ut.us

Vermont
Ed Von Turkovich, Director
Department of Public Safety
e-mail: evonturk@dps.state.vt.us

Virginia
Michael Cline, Director
Department of Public Safety
e-mail: mcline.des@state.va.us

Washington
Glen Woodbury, Director
Military Services Division
e-mail: g.woodbury@emd.wa.gov

West Virginia
John Pack Jr., Director
Military Department
e-mail: dirwvoes@mail.wvnet.edu

Wisconsin
Steven Sell, Director
Military Department
e-mail: sells@dma.state.wi.us

Wyoming
Robert Bezek, Director
Military Department
e-mail: bezekb@wy.iso.army.mil

Puerto Rico
Epifano Jimenez Melendez, Director
State Civil Defense
e-mail: epifaniojimenez@prct.net

BUSINESS, CONSUMER, AND GOVERNMENT INFORMATION RESOURCES

Business and Industry

Federal Reserve Bank Guide for Small Businesses
http://www.frbsf.org/fiservices/cdc/smallbus/index.html
The Century Date Change Project provides a guidance document for small businesses.

Frequently Asked Questions (FAQ)
http://www.computerpro.com/~phystad/csy2kfaq.html
Regularly updated, this detailed document defines the Y2K problem, discusses its social and historical implications, describes specific hardware and software issues, gives examples of how to fix the problem, and provides links to additional resources and tools.

Industry Search (NorthernLight)
http://www.northernlight.com/industry.html
Type "y2k" or "millennium bug" or "century date change" in the Search For box, and select an industry or "All Industries" to find articles on how business is managing Y2K.

Information Technology Association of America (ITAA)
http://www.itaa.org/year2000/index.htm
ITAA, an authoritative voice addressing the year 2000 issue, presents information from its Year 2000 Task Group, which consists of computer software and services vendors. The scope extends beyond the federal marketplace to firms interested in troubleshooting in state and local commercial sectors.

National Association of Manufacturers Clearinghouse for Current Solutions
http://www.nam.org/y2k/y2khome.asp
This trade association helps small and medium-size firms share information about products and services dealing with the year 2000 problem. To search the site, key in the name or type of company.

Prudential Small Business Guide
http://www.prudential.com/corporate/techatpru/y2k/cotyzl000.html
A three-step plan and worksheets to help small businesses address the year 2000 problem.

Small Business Administration (SBA)
http://www.sba.gov/y2k
Presents links to recommended steps, checklists, and solution providers to help small businesses identify and correct the Y2K problem.

Consumer

Banking
http://www.fdic.gov/about/y2k
The Federal Deposit Insurance Corporation (FDIC) provides information on insured deposits, as well as articles such as "Is Your Money Safe?" "Y2K Fixes and Frauds," and "A Bank Customer's 'To Do' List."

Consumer Electronics
http://www.cemacity.org/govt/CEMA2000.htm
Lists Y2K-compliant appliance manufacturers.

Government Hotlines
http://www.nist.gov/y2k/consumer.htm
Provides links to US government telephone hotlines for consumer and small-business information on Y2K.

Investor Kit
http://www. nasdr.com/3600_inv_kit.htm
The Securities and Exchange Commission (SEC), the National Association of Securities Dealers, and the Securities Industry Association offer an "Investor Kit" to help investors deal with Y2K, together with a review of the financial industry's preparatory efforts. The kit includes a list of questions frequently asked by investors, as well as a Y2K checklist.

Mitre and Y2K
http://www.mitre.org/research/y2k
Addresses year 2000 education, tools, and methods—a repository of critical information.

Y2Kbase
http://www.y2kbase.com
A comprehensive independent database providing search and browse features for finding Y2K-compliant products and services.

Federal Government

CIO Council Year 2000 Information Directory
http://www.itpolicy.gsa.gov/mks/yr2000/y2khome.htm
General Services Administration's directory provides up-to-date information as well as links to federal and state Y2K Web sites.

Department of Housing and Urban Development Y2K Site
http://www.hud.gov/cio/year2000/

Department of Treasury Y2K Site
http://www.treas.gov/y2k/

Environmental Protection Agency Year 2000 Site
http://www.epa.gov/year2000/index.htm

FDIC Year 2000 Project
http://www.fdic.gov/about/y2k/
Presents information on financial institutions and the work they are doing to bring their computer systems into compliance.

Federal Aviation Administration's Year 2000 Site
http://www.faay2k.com/

Federal Communications Commission Year 2000 Page
http://www.fcc.gov/year2000/
Provides information to communications and broadcasting companies, and customers, who are interested in FCC and industry activities.

Federal Highway Administration Year 2000 Site
http://www.fhwa.dot.gov/y2k/index.htm

Food Supply Information from USDA
http://www.usda.gov/aphis/FSWG/grocery.html
Posts links to grocery and convenience stores that are working on Y2K complications.

General Accounting Office: GAO Reports and Publications
http://www.gao.gov/y2kr.htm
Since February 1997, GAO has written dozens of reports on the government's response to Y2K, and on specific federal agencies' readiness to handle it. Included are assessment and testing guides, as well as a manual for business continuity and contingency planning.

General Services Administration
http://www.itpolicy.gsa.gov/mks/yr2000/y201toc1.htm
Posts links to international, consumer, and communiy information, including Y2K for kids.

General Services Administration Y2K Telecommunications Site
http://y2k.fts.gsa.gov/
Provides the latest Y2K compliance information about products and services for federal, state, local, and tribal government telecommunications managers.

Health Care Financing Administration Y2K Site
http://www.hcfa.gov/y2k/
Presents information on Medicare and Medicaid systems.

National Association of Counties Y2K Information
http://www.naco.org/programs/infotech/y2k/sites.cfm
Offers a county program section, tool kit, vendor list, assessment survey, discussion forum, as well as links to related sites and relevant articles.

National Institute of Standards and Technology Year 2000 Page
http://www.nist.gov/y2k/index.htm
The National Institute of Standards and Technology's Information Technology Laboratory (ITL) offers testing and standards for testing year 2000 features.

National Weather Service Y2K Information and Testing
http://www.oso1.x3.nws.noaa.gov/y2k/
Provides news, notices, plans, tests, software utilities, and more from the National Weather Service Office of Systems Operation.

Nuclear Regulatory Commission (NRC) Y2K Planning
http://www.nrc.gov/NRC/NEWS/year2000.html
Presents a comprehensive program for dealing with the Y2K problem.

Office of Management and Budget Year 2000 Progress Report
http://www.cio.gov/598rpt.html
The report summarizes federal actions taken to address the year 2000 problem.

President's Council on the Year 2000 Conversion
http://www.y2k.gov/java/index.htm
The Council, established on February 4, 1998, by Executive Order 13073, is responsible for coordinating the federal government's response to the Y2K problem.

Securities Exchange Commission Year 2000 Page
http://www.sec.gov/news/home2000.htm
Addresses computer systems compliance pertaining to internal systems and market regulation.

Social Security Administration Y2K Information
http://www.ssa.gov/facts/y2knotic.html

US Department of Education Year 2000 Page
http://www.ed.gov/offices/OCIO/year/
Addresses the utility and preservation of information systems for educational facilities.

U.S. Federal Government Gateway for Year 2000 Information Directories
http://www.itpolicy.gsa.gov/mks/yr2000/y2khome.htm
Posts links to official US government sources for information on the Y2K problem.

International Government

Action 2000
http://www.bug2000.co.uk/index2.shtml
Helps businesses in the United Kingdom deal with the Y2K problem, and provides information on the status of government and business compliance.

International Y2K Cooperation Center (IY2KCC)
http://www.iy2kcc.org
The IY2KCC, established in February 1999 under United Nations auspices, with World Bank funding, links national Y2K coordinators from over 150 countries and provides information about Y2K "best practices." It also sponsors the Y2K Expert Service (YES) Volunteer Corps, an international network of volunteers prepared to help countries in need of technical assistance.

Y2K Task Force for Canadian Government/Industry
http://strategis.ic.gc.ca/sc_mangb/y2k/engdoc/homepage.html
Assists Canadians in dealing with the year 2000 computer problem.

ABOUT THE AUTHORS

JEFFEREY MODIC, a respected authority on information management, has spent the past twenty-five years advising public and private organizations on the strategic management of their information resources and technology. He first began to address the year 2000 computer-date problem as a systems engineer at Electronic Data Systems in 1976. Since then, he has lectured and written about its far-reaching impact on society, government, and business. He has also served as a course instructor at several educational institutes, including George Washington University in Washington, DC. Currently, he is president of American Information Engineering Corporation, an information management services company.

Jeff lives with his wife Susan and their two young children in Tres Pinos, California, a small ranching community near Silicon Valley. From there he assists city, county, state, and federal officials in Y2K contingency planning, emergency response planning, and community preparedness programs. He is also the author of *The Reasonable Person's Guide to Y2K* (Tres Pinos Press, 1999).

BAYARD STOCKTON, winner of Associated Press awards for documentary and commentary, is a former foreign correspondent for *Newsweek,* ABC, BBC, and German radio and TV. Now a writer, editor, and writing teacher in Santa Barbara, California, he is the author of *Phoenix with a Bayonet* (Georgetown Publishers, 1971), *Oceans of Gold* (privately published), and *Catapult: The Biography of Robert A. Monroe* (Donning, 1988).

TO THE READER

You have many choices when it comes to books, which is why I want to thank you for taking the time to read *Nothing to Fear.* I hope you enjoyed reading it as much as I enjoyed creating it.

I would like to hear your comments about this novel, or about issues or questions it raises for you. I would also like to receive any helpful suggestions you might have for living with Y2K's aftereffects in the new millennium. Please e-mail your thoughts and suggestions directly to:

jmodic@trespinos.com.

I have written another book, entitled *The Reasonable Person's Guide to Y2K.* This volume, geared to families, friends, and communities, addresses some of the most frequently asked questions about year 2000. Although you cannot purchase this book, I am happy to provide you with a free copy as a way of saying thank you for reading *Nothing to Fear.* Simply e-mail your request to Tres Pinos Press at: publisher@trespinos.com. Type "Free Guide" in the message area. Orders will be filled on a first-come basis.

I look forward to hearing from you . . . real soon.

Jefferey Modic
Tres Pinos Press
www.trespinos.com

SPECIAL OFFER

Nothing to Fear is currently available at local bookstores for $16.00. However, if you would like to receive a *signed edition* for your library or to give to friends and family, kindly fill out the form on the facing page and mail or fax it to Tres Pinos Press. You can also place your order on our Web site.

This offer is available to individual purchasers only, not to wholesalers or resellers. Requests are processed in the order in which they are received.

ORDER FORM

Nothing to Fear	Qty.	Price per Unit	Total
1–7 signed books		$16.00	
8–14 signed books		$14.50	
15+ signed books		$13.00	
		Subtotal	
	California residents, add 7.25% sales tax		
		Total	

* Shipping is free within the continental US.

For orders outside the continental US, add $10.00 shipping & handling per book.

Name:	Please select payment option:
Street:	❏ Check enclosed for $_____(US) Made payable to **Tres Pinos Press**
City/State/Zip:	❏ VISA ❏ MasterCard
Phone: ( )	Credit card #:
Fax: ( )	Expiration date:
e-mail:	Authorized signature:

Tres Pinos Press
PO Box 1174
Tres Pinos, CA 95075
Fax: 831-628-3863
Web site: www.trespinos.com